THE
CAVALIER OF
RABBIT BUTTE

Center Point
Large Print

Also by Robert J. Horton and available from Center Point Large Print:

Man of the Desert

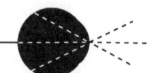

**This Large Print Book carries the
Seal of Approval of N.A.V.H.**

THE
CAVALIER OF
RABBIT BUTTE

Robert J. Horton

CENTER POINT LARGE PRINT
THORNDIKE, MAINE

This Center Point Large Print edition is published
in the year 2014 by arrangement with
Golden West Literary Agency.

The text of this Large Print edition is unabridged.
In other aspects, this book may vary from the original edition.
Printed in the United States of America on permanent paper.
Set in 16-point Times New Roman type.

ISBN: 978-1-62899-381-3 (hardcover)
ISBN: 978-1-62899-387-5 (softcover)

Library of Congress Cataloging-in-Publication Data

Horton, Robert J., 1881–1934.
 The cavalier of Rabbit Butte : a western story / Robert J. Horton. —
Center Point Large Print edition.
 pages ; cm
 Summary: "Steve Brent's cavalier attitude makes him look suspicious
when lawmen are looking for rustlers and bank robbers"—Provided by
publisher.
 ISBN 978-1-62899-381-3 (hardcover : alk. paper)
 ISBN 978-1-62899-387-5 (pbk. : alk. paper)
 1. Large type books. I. Title.
 PS3515.O745C38 2014
 813'.52—dc23
                                                    2014035893

Contents

CHAPTER ONE
A Man of Words

Man and horse wore an air of weariness as they broke through the trees along the river and struck west into a sea of gray bunch grass. The man pulled down the brim of his hat against the bright rays of the early morning sun and, twisting in the saddle, scanned the prairie to eastward. It was bare and endless. In the north, a series of low buttes showed like pin points beyond a vast waste of plain. He looked toward the blue mountains in the west and shook out the bridle reins.

The horse broke into a lope. It was a homely beast—tall, bony, long necked, rather peaked in the face and muzzle—a cross between a dun and a sorrel. It was such a horse as a self-respecting cow-puncher would shoot at first sight, rather than turn in with his string. But the animal's appearance belied its performance, for, though obviously ridden through the night, the gelding carried on tirelessly across the bunch grass.

The rider, by crude comparison, presented a different aspect. He was tall, slim but well-muscled, as his movements attested; gray-eyed, firm-lipped, square of chin, with a clean skin stung a dull bronze by wind and sun. He might have been twenty-five or thirty-five; when his

7

eyes twinkled, as they did by spells for no apparent reason, he appeared to be the former age; when he squinted in long-distance gaze he seemed the latter.

His hat, shirt, boots, and chaps displayed the unmistakable signs of travel; but the butt of the gun in the holster at his right side was free of dust as though it had been fondled often in the course of the long ride.

As they left the river behind, the rider's interest in the country increased. He grunted in satisfaction when he saw, finally, a herd of cattle grazing on the open range to northward. He pushed back his hat and swung his right foot free of the stirrup—an infallible sign of contentment on the part of a rider—when he descried a clump of willows about a tall, stately cottonwood straight ahead in the west.

"Hoss, prick up your ears," he said aloud; "where there's willows an' a tree that a way ahead there, there's a spring. An' where there's a spring there's bound to be cattle close. An' where there's cattle, there's liable to be habitations. We see the spring an' the stock, an' I reckon we're on the right track, hoss. Put 'em down a little faster—let's slope!"

The horse increased its pace as if it understood its master's logic. In half an hour, they reached the willows and the tree and found a deep, natural spring, or slough, with banks trodden by cattle and horses.

The horse refused to drink, for it had been watered at the river, and the man sat his saddle and looked about him. His interest centered on the trunk of the tall cottonwood. A square of white gleamed against the gray bark. He dismounted, stepped to the tree, stood with legs braced well apart, his hands on his hips, and read a printed notice.

REWARD!

For the capture of LONG PETE, dead or alive, two thousand dollars. For any of his gang, five hundred dollars each. For the outfit, five thousand dollars will be paid in cash.

JAMES LYNCH, Banker.
ED FURNESS, Sheriff.
Rangeview, Rabbit Butte County.

The rider read the notice through twice, stepped away from the tree and squinted at it.

"That's what I call a right generous, easy-to-understand offer," he said in a hearty voice. "Two thousand for the old sport himself, five hundred for any of his playmates, or five thousand for corrallin' the bunch. Everything there except their descriptions an' what they're wanted for!"

He grinned and went back to his horse. He swung into the saddle and leaned thoughtfully on the horn.

"Now, hoss, the way to make money on a deal like that would be to capture or kill Long Pete's cohorts one by one, collectin' five hundred a head, an' leaving the old boy till the last for a clean-up of two thousand. If he had twenty men with him, let's see, that would be—"

"Throw 'em up—*way up!*" The command came from behind, and the rider raised his hands above his head.

"All right, stranger," he sang out, "but it's shore an ignominious proceedin' any way you look at it, an'—"

"Shut up an' keep 'em up there," came the order as a man walked from the screen of willows into sight near the head of the horse. He was tall and spare, black-eyed, with a long nose and a bristly mustache; swarthy of skin, thin-lipped, scowling. He wore town clothes, riding boots and a derby —a black derby hat. He covered the man on the horse with a forty-five.

"What do you think of that notice?" he asked sharply.

"I was just thinkin' to myself that it's one of the plainest notices I ever saw," was the drawling reply. "There can't be any mistake about the amounts—they're all set out clear an' exact. I reckon Long Pete himself couldn't kick at that notice—'specially since it don't tell what he looks like."

"What's your name?"

"Brent—Steve Brent. I'm actually givin' you my real name, Sheriff."

The other man's eyes widened a bit. "What makes you think I'm a sheriff?" he inquired in a tone of suspicious surprise.

"I heard south of here that there was a tough sheriff up here that wore one of them derbies," was the cheerful rejoinder. "I was right curious to meet you, Sheriff, but I didn't figure I'd meet you just when I needed to meet somebody who could wise me up as to the proper direction to take to get to town."

The other's gun hand wavered ever so little. "I wear a derby hat because I like 'em," he said in a voice that suggested he might be pleased because of Brent's reference to him as being tough; "but I'm not out here to give directions to strangers that's travelin' light an' far. You've been ridin' quite a piece, I take it."

"You're Ed Furness then, for shore?" asked Brent.

"Yes, I'm Ed Furness," said the other, his scowl deepening. "I don't know why I should be tellin' you."

"Well, Ed, it's this way"—Brent's tone was earnest—"I have rode quite a piece, an' my hoss an' me are lookin' for something in the way of a town, where we can put up an' hang on the nose bag an' rest a spell, an'—"

"Your horse looks as though he needed a

powerful lot of both them things you mentioned," the sheriff broke in with a faint smile. "Don't know if he'd make it to Rangeview or not."

"How far is it, Ed?"

"Now don't lay down too heavy on that Ed stuff," said the sheriff tartly. "You ain't acquainted with me much yet. But you're liable to be, if you can't give a good account of yourself."

"Ain't you forgettin' somethin', Sheriff?"

"Not as I know of, an' I don't intend to, if I can help it."

"I still got my hands up, Sheriff, an' I'm pretty tired."

The sheriff's gun stiffened in his hand to a full bead on Brent's heart. "You can put your left hand down. Just keep the other up a minute." He stepped around the horse to Brent's right and drew the latter's weapon from its holster. "You can ease your right now."

"Say, Sheriff," said Brent in a confidential tone that quickened the official's ear, "I just saved your life!"

"Go ahead, I'm ready for it—I'll bite," said Furness. "But I know what you're going to say. You're going to tell me that you could have pulled your gun an' plugged me while I was walkin' aroun' the horse."

Brent leaned back in his saddle with a look of admiration on his face.

"S'help me, Sheriff, that was just what I was

goin' to say. I didn't think you'd comprehend what I was gettin' at so quick."

"You spill a lot of big words," the sheriff observed.

"I've got twenty of 'em," Brent confessed; "an even twenty. I've all but got 'em numbered. I had a school-marm down on the Musselshell once, an' she taught 'em to me. The word *comprehend* was the second one she taught me—so it's number two."

"It won't do you any good to spill 'em on me," scowled the sheriff.

"I sling 'em naturally," said Brent with an easy gesture. "But I wasn't kiddin' about bein' able to draw when you stepped past that hoss's head. I meant that!"

His quick gaze met the sheriff's—cool and convincing. Ed Furness showed by his manner that he was puzzled. "What's your business up here?" he asked finally.

"I come up here for a change of range, Sheriff." Brent leaned on his saddle horn. "I've worked cows, an' I've flirted with the blue checks. But I've never sneered at the white ones. I'm a restless spirit. I figured I'd come up in this north country an' see what it looked like an' maybe hook on to a job somewheres. I was goin' on into the first town I saw, if my hoss could make it. But the first thing I see is a reward notice an' the second is a sheriff. I reckon this country is plumb unfriendly."

The sheriff's scowl returned. "You want to go to Rangeview?"

"If that's the nearest town, that's where I want to go."

"It's the only town within a hundred miles or so," said the sheriff, half to himself; "an' I guess I could get you any time I wanted you. I been watching this spring, but I been lookin' for somebody from the north. You don't look so bad to me, even if you can sling a gun like you say. Maybe you could have done what you said you could when I stepped aroun' the horse, but I dunno. I expected you to try it."

Steve Brent's teeth flashed white against his tan in a broad smile. "Ed, I reckon you're the goods, but I didn't intend to try it. That notice don't bother me none. It's the first time I ever heard of Long Pete or his gang. You can look in my slicker pack behind on the saddle an' you won't find nary a thing but a spare shirt or two, some socks, a few sacks of tobacco, an' some knickknacks I carry aroun' for—sentimental reasons. That's another of my words, Sheriff. But if you want to take me in, let's start, for I'm hungrier than a steer in February."

Sheriff Furness looked at him steadily for a full minute. Then he looked at the horse, and his gaze changed to one of pity. He pointed west with his gun.

"Rangeview's eleven miles straight as a string

in that direction," he said slowly. "You can go on in, an' I'll be following you shortly. When I come in I'll give you your gun—providin' you haven't attracted too much unfavorable attention. You better walk an' lead your horse. You're liable to bust him down."

"Thanks, Sheriff," said Brent, grinning, "but I can't walk. I'm too—I'm too—ungainly."

He touched his mount lightly with his spurs, and as he started, he called back: "Don't forget about the gun, Sheriff; I feel totally undressed!"

He rode through the willows and out into the sea of bunch grass.

"Talked him out of it, hoss," he sang in a low, vibrant voice. "Let's beat it for the oat bin."

His mount broke into a swinging lope, and they headed straight for town.

CHAPTER TWO
A Forced Loan

It was barely nine o'clock when Steve Brent rode jauntily into Rangeview; that is, Brent bore himself in a jaunty manner, but his horse walked slowly, with hanging head, seemingly on the point of collapse.

Rangeview was a typical old cow town. The buildings on either side of its short main street were sadly weatherbeaten, with false fronts, suggesting a second story that didn't exist, and which had long since lost the brilliancy of their illusion through the cracking and peeling of paint. The street was nothing but a road, and filled with dust. The hitching rails were grooved where ropes and reins had worn into the wood. The glass in the windows was a dull opaque, almost impervious to light. It was a drab perspective save for the green of the cottonwoods, which grew in profusion, and a number of freshly painted signs left as blazes on the trail of some itinerant artist.

Brent was riding slowly along the street, looking for the livery stable where he could put up his horse, when he heard a hail. He saw a man approaching from in front of one of the more pretentious buildings. He was a portly man, displaying an ample expanse of vest and watch

16

chain, red-faced, with heavy jowls, brown of eye with a gray mustache and bushy gray brows. He wore a gray suit, a white collar with a string tie, and a stockman's hat of very light tan.

He stopped close to Brent and looked up at him, throwing his head well back and hooking his thumbs in the armholes of his vest.

"Stranger here?" he asked in a heavy voice.

Brent lifted his right foot from the stirrup and leaned with his left forearm on the horn. He regarded his interrogator gravely. "Do you live here?" he asked pleasantly.

The bushy, gray brows came together in a frown. "You'll do better to answer questions instead of ask 'em, young man, coming in here on a spent horse an' the dust of three counties on your shirt. We're not partial to strangers here these days."

"Shucks! I expect I'm unlucky that a way," said Brent. "Always askin' questions. Where's the livery barn?"

The other glared at him for a few moments, and then his gaze roved over Brent's mount. "You're not going to the expense of puttin' that horse in a barn to die, are you? Haw, haw! Say, young fellow, are you lookin' for a job?"

"I'm lookin' for the livery barn," said Brent easily; "an' I don't reckon this town is so big but what I'll find it."

"You watch your knitting or you may find this

town too big," said the large man with a scowl. "I see you're not packing a gun. Well, that's a peaceful sign, unless somebody took it away from you. Do you know anything about cows?"

"My friend," said Brent slowly, "it pains me to think what I've forgotten about cows—an' I've got a powerful good memory."

"Meaning you're a top hand?" asked the other with fresh interest. "If you are, I'll give you a job."

"Well, now, that's right kind of you," Brent drawled out. "I had thought some of goin' to work up here, but I figured it would take me a day or two to pick my outfit. I'm particular that a way. There's outfits that couldn't hire me at any price, an' there's outfits I'd almost work for for nothing. I'm peculiar that a way. I've got to be in good company."

"I have the largest outfit in this country," boasted the big man. "I own the Rabbit Foot."

"Say, this country sort of runs to rabbits, don't it?" asked Brent with an innocent expression on his face. "This is Rabbit Butte County, an' yours is the Rabbit Foot outfit. I reckon it ought to be lucky, eh?"

The other appeared undecided as to whether this was intended as a joke or not. He looked Brent over appraisingly. "I'll give you fifty dollars a month to start," he said, nodding his head and smiling affably. "That's five dollars a month more than the usual starting wages. You can go out this afternoon."

Brent scratched his head and appeared bewildered. "That's all right. I know you're surprised," said the large man; "but I guess I can spot a cow hand when I see him, an' I'm banking on my judgment in your case."

"I'm tryin' to figure out what I'd ever do with that extra five dollars a month," Brent explained.

"You're smart, that's the trouble with you. Well, listen to me, I'm James Lynch, owner of the Rabbit Foot and that bank over there. I'm a good man to work for, I am. You can't do better up here."

"So you're James Lynch," said Brent, leaning down for a closer view of the other's face. "Well, Jim, I read your notice an' I met Ed back there a piece. What you got against Long Pete?"

Lynch's jaw dropped for an instant. "You mean Ed Furness, the sheriff? Don't you know who Long Pete is?"

"Yes an' no; that answers both of 'em," replied Brent.

"Long Pete's the worst rustler that ever worked in here," said Lynch, his face darkening. "I'd pay those rewards myself if I could get him and his gang. I'll pay half of 'em, anyway. But he'll be hard to catch, for we don't know what he looks like. Where'd you say you saw Ed Furness?"

"Back by the big spring," Brent answered with a

yawn. "I reckon he's figurin' on Long Pete showin' up there to get a drink. Well, Jim, I got to put my hoss up an' get a bite an' a few winks of sleep. So long."

"Wait a minute!" Lynch commanded. "Are you going to take that job an' do business with me?"

"I don't guess I want your job, but I might want to do business with you at your bank," said Brent. "I might want to borrow some money, if you've got any to lend."

"You can borrow money from me any day if you've got any security," said Lynch in a sneering tone. "If you want to go to work for me and are broke, I'll advance you a month's wages."

"I might give you my hoss for security," said Brent, smiling.

"Your horse! Haw, haw, haw! Well, young fellow, in the first place that ain't a horse, but whatever it is, I couldn't let you have more'n five hundred on it. Haw, haw, haw!"

The banker wiped his eyes as though his mirth was real instead of simulated.

"I reckon that would be enough," said Brent with a grim smile. "So long."

"You better think over that job, if you're going to hang around here," Lynch called after him as he rode down the street.

Brent found the barn at the farther end of the street and put up his horse, giving explicit directions as to the animal's care and waiting to see that they were carried out. Then he went to the hotel, ate breakfast, and retired to a room, requesting that he be called in six hours.

It was half past three in the afternoon when he was awakened. He went at once to the barn.

"Pretty well done up," said the barn man, referring to Brent's horse.

"I reckon he needs rest," Brent admitted. "I plan on leavin' him here a spell. Don't forget his name is Hunchy, an' that my name is Brent—Steve Brent. That's Steve Brent's hoss, Hunchy."

"I ain't the forgettin' kind," answered the barn man, grinning.

A third man came swaggering into the barn. He was a large, swarthy man, dressed in leather chaps, Mackinaw shirt, riding boots sadly in need of cleaning, and wore a huge, wide-brimmed hat, pushed far back on his head.

"Why don't you buy a *real* horse?" he blustered out.

"What makes you think I want to buy a hoss?" Brent asked mildly.

"Why, you ain't got none," said the other with a loud laugh. "I seen what you brought in." The whole barn echoed with his roaring laugh, as he nudged the barn man.

"You got a hoss to sell?" Brent put the question quietly.

"Sure. I'll sell any horse I've got if I can get enough for him." The man looked Brent over with

21

a deprecating grin. "C'mon an' look at this one."

He led the way to a corral at the rear of the barn, pointed out a beautiful black gelding, fully fourteen hands high. Every line of the animal suggested speed and endurance. He paced about the corral with impatience. He had a good eye, and Brent veiled his gaze of admiration. Here was a horse in a thousand for spirit.

"There y'are," said the dark-faced man. "You can have that horse for five hundred.

"How soon do I have to pay the money?" asked Brent almost in a whisper.

"Oh, you ain't got it, eh? I thought so. Goin' out to rustle it? I'll give you till six o'clock. Hear that, Jake?" The big man turned to the barn man. "If he brings in five hundred by six o'clock, sell him the horse. But remember, I'm startin' back for the ranch 'bout six one." He left the barn chuckling.

The barn man, Jake, smiled. "He's worth it, Brent. But it's too much to pay for a horse in this country. Your horse will be all right in another day. He's got more in him than most of 'em think."

Brent nodded. "Who was that fellow?" he asked.

"That's Bill Lawton, foreman out at the Rabbit Foot."

Brent grew thoughtful. "Put my saddle an' bridle on that hoss," he said after a time. "If I ain't back for him by six you can take it off an' nobody'll be any wiser. If I come back an' hand you five hundred, well—you know the deal."

Brent left the barn and walked up the street. Almost the first man he met was Sheriff Ed Furness. The sheriff greeted him almost cordially.

"Step in here to the justice's office," he invited.

They entered a little, one-story building, and the sheriff opened a drawer of the desk in the center of the front room. He took out Brent's gun and handed it to him.

"You said your name was Brent? All right. Brent, if I was you, I'd go over to Lynch's bank and do business with him." There was a veiled command in the sheriff's tone.

"Maybe you're right, Ed," drawled out Brent. "It seems right nice to have so many folks round here interested in a wanderin' cow hand. I may do that very little thing."

He left the sheriff with a queer smile and proceeded across the street and back down to the State Bank of Rangeview. When he entered he saw a small cage in the front of the room and a private room in the rear. The door to the private room in the rear was open. This was unoccupied. But there was a man in the cage, evidently a clerk. Lynch was not in sight. Brent stepped to the window of the cage over which appeared the word "cashier" in brass letters.

"Let me have a note blank, please," he said in a soft voice.

"For yourself?" asked the clerk, staring at Brent through thick lenses.

"Yes," replied Brent quietly.

"Have you an account here?" asked the clerk politely. It was evident he did not know all the bank's customers and was inclined to treat Brent with respect.

"No, I have no account." Brent frowned. "An' I haven't much time."

"It's against the rules," said the clerk. "I—"

"Can anybody take one of your note blanks out an' get money on it?" asked Brent.

"No—of course not." The clerk hesitated.

"Then hand one over," Brent commanded. "Jim Lynch an' I have already had some talk about this."

At mention of the banker's name, the clerk readily complied with the request and pushed a note form through under the wire network.

Brent took the blank, stepped to the wall desk, and quickly filled it out. He returned to the window and slipped it through.

"Give me the money on that," he said briskly.

The clerk looked at the note and smiled uneasily. "I can't give you five hundred on this. I don't know about the security, and Mr. Lynch has to approve all loans."

"The security is my hoss, Hunchy," said Brent. "He's in the barn below here. Jim Lynch told me just this mornin' that he couldn't loan more'n five hundred on my hoss, an' that's all I'm askin'."

"But—"

The one word was all the clerk was able to speak. There was a quick movement of Brent's right hand and forearm and the bank employee found himself staring into the black bore of a six-shooter. His face went white.

"In fair-sized bills—an' quick!" said Brent sharply.

The clerk looked for an instant into Brent's eyes. His hands trembled as he counted out the money.

"Now beat it back into that room behind there," Brent ordered, stuffing the bills in his hat and putting the hat back on his head. "I told you once I didn't have much time. Do you think I'm foolin'?"

The clerk backed toward the rear room with Brent walking along on the outside of the cage, keeping him covered. At the farther end of the cage was a door.

"Unlatch it!" Brent snapped out.

The clerk complied and Brent entered the cage. In a few moments he had locked the clerk in a closet off the rear room. Then he hurried out of the building and walked rapidly to the barn. He thrust the bills into Jake's hands.

"Count 'em," he said with an easy smile; "an' I'll be on my way."

He went out to the corral and found the big black saddled and bridled. He led him out as the barn man approached. "All here," said Jake, "but—"

"So long," sang Brent as he swung into the saddle. "Give my regards to Jim an' Ed an' Bill Lawton, an' take good care of Hunchy."

With that he tickled the black with his spurs and swept out under the trees to the open prairie. The big black snorted, tossed his head, and struck west at a ringing gallop toward the mountains, running red with the blood of the dying day.

CHAPTER THREE

Cornered

Brent saw a low butte some miles ahead in the west and rode in that direction. Before he reached the vicinity of the butte, however, he saw cattle and a group of ranch buildings. The buildings were in the center of a large plot of ground seeded to grain, evidently well watered, to the south of the butte.

"I wonder now if we're headed for Rabbit Butte an' the Rabbit Foot Ranch," he muttered to himself, scanning the lay of the land.

There were some riders with the cattle and two of these started out to meet him. He turned north, intending to ride around the north end of the butte. But the riders approaching had no intention of permitting him to continue on his way until they had talked with him. They cut north to head him off. Brent let the black out and raced for the north end of the butte toward what was apparently open country, though broken by coulees and miniature ridges where there was a growth of scrub pine and considerable buck brush.

"I reckon we're goin' to look this country over in our own way," said Brent to the horse. "An' it's mighty queer those fellows would be so much interested in a rider comin' along unless—well, if anybody knows what Long Pete looks like, they're maybe givin' every hombre the once-over that hits these parts. Just the same, delays ain't what we want right now."

The big black was rapidly outdistancing the pair of riders coming from the south when Brent became aware of a new factor in the situation. Glances behind him to eastward disclosed other mounted men approaching from that direction.

"They've woke up in town," he said with concern. "Hoss, you'll have to step!"

There was no doubt in his mind as he spurred the black but that the riders in the east were a sheriff's posse, led, probably, by Ed Furness himself. Bill Lawton likely was with him. Whether or not they could tell who he was at that distance he did not know; but he decided to take no chances. He called on the black horse for everything he had, and the magnificent animal fairly flew over the ground, straight north.

The sun had gone down and the first blue shades of the twilight were drifting across the land. The prairie wind was freshening—sure harbinger of night. Brent took advantage of everything in the way of trees, brush, and rises of ground to screen the movements of himself and horse. He saw the two riders in the south stop in the gathering shadows and then turn back. The riders in the east were evidently cutting due west to the ranch.

Brent veered into the northwest. He now was

north and east of the butte. Soon he reached the broken country that reached to the foothills of the mountains. Here he found it necessary to slow his paces but he soon was aware that the horse he rode knew something of the country.

"Must be that Bill Lawton's been ridin' in here," he thought. "If that's the Rabbit Foot south of the butte it stands to reason that Bill's job as foreman would take him up here now an' then to look over the range. Funny there are no cattle up here. Good grass."

He struck a wide, hard trail leading into the heart of the tumbled country and followed it. As he rode in and out of coulees, through long ravines, over ridges and across patches of meadow and gravel, with the scrub pines waving their short, grotesque arms on either side, he hummed a song.

"I'm ole Steve Brent, an' on trouble I'm bent,
Expectin' to find it in bunches;
I'll find it, you bet, for I've never failed yet,
When playin' a pair of my hunches."

The song was obviously original, and Brent evidently liked it, for he sang it time after time. The shades of night deepened and the first stars pierced the velvet canopy of the sky with pin points of light that gradually expanded and increased until the heavens swarmed with constellations.

Brent rode free with the wind in his face, humming his verse, but keeping a sharp lookout by the light of the stars along the trail ahead.

"Looks like we camp out to-night, hoss," he said cheerfully. "But I reckon that ain't nothing new to either of us. I forgot to ask your name, but you sure appreciate bein' rid by someone who knows the feel of saddle leather."

He ceased his prattle and drew rein as he glimpsed a light ahead. It was a steady, yellow light such as would shine from a window— lamplight. He proceeded cautiously until he reached the edge of a small meadow in the center of which was a cabin. He could see a small shed or barn behind the cabin and some corrals. The light was shining from a single window on the side of the cabin toward him, but another beam, lower and longer, from the end of the house indicated that a door was open.

He circled the meadow on the side opposite the door and found the shed and corrals empty. He shrugged his shoulders in sudden decision and rode swiftly around to the door. As he pulled up in the beam of light a boy appeared in the door.

"Who's there?"

"Why, sonny, I reckon it's me," sang Brent, dismounting and stepping into the light where he could see the boy and be seen himself.

The youth looked at him searchingly out of wide, dark eyes.

"You from the ranch?" he asked.

"I'm from a couple dozen ranches, son, but if you're meanin' the one below the butte, I'll say no an' ask you what place it is."

A glance into the lighted room of the cabin showed Brent that it was unoccupied.

"That's the Rabbit Foot down there," the boy said wonderingly. "You a stranger?"

"I'm that an' more," replied Brent with a smile. "I'm a hungry stranger, son, an' your light looked plumb friendly."

"Put your horse in the shed," said the boy, "an' come in an' eat."

"Those are true words of hospitality," approved Steve Brent. "An' it's good advice in the bargain. I'll do those things pronto."

He put up his horse and entered the cabin. The boy was at the stove.

"There's the wash bench," he said, pointing to bench, wash dish, and a pail of water beside the door. "If you won't want to use it, you don't have to; but Pa says a man eats better with a clean face."

"Words of wisdom," said Brent with a friendly smile. "Your pa has some good ideas."

Brent looked at the boy closely. He was a good-looking youngster, about fourteen years old, a bit dark, clear skinned with clean-cut features, brown eyes and a shock of tousled, chestnut hair. He was well built and would one day be a large,

31

powerful man. He wore riding boots, faded blue overalls, and a light-gray flannel shirt, evidently made over from one of his father's.

"What's your name, son?" Brent asked when he had finished washing.

"Alan," the boy answered with a flashing smile; "Alan Carman."

"That's a good name," Brent observed soberly. "Mine's Steve Brent. I reckon we ought to get along."

"Don't see many folks in here," said the boy with a wide gaze. "You—traveling far?"

"Well, that'll depend," Brent evaded. "I'll maybe have to ask some questions 'bout this country in here. I sort of stumbled in."

The boy listened intently while Brent rambled on telling of the south range, of Texas, of the sheep wars; putting a question now and then about the surrounding country and getting a satisfactory answer. In this way Brent learned that Rabbit Foot cattle were not ranged north of the butte; in fact, Lynch, who owned the big ranch, had had a fence strung across the north end of the butte, shutting off the tumbled lands. There was no town for nearly a hundred miles north to the main line of the railroad. The boy didn't know where his father had gone.

When it came time to turn in, Alan took Brent into the bedroom of the cabin where there were two bunks. Brent was invited to sleep in the elder

Carman's bunk. The boy volunteered the information that his mother had been dead since before he could remember, and that his father was his only living relative so far as he knew. He had no boy companions and had had very little schooling.

They talked in the darkness after they had gone to bed. When they finally dozed off it seemed to Brent that he had hardly closed his eyes when he was wide awake listening to sounds outside the cabin. He heard the youth stirring. Then came a loud knocking on the outside door.

"Who's there?" called the youth.

"Open up!" came the command.

Brent got out of the bunk and hastily pulled on his clothes in the darkness as the boy moved into the other room.

"I don't intend to open up till I know who's there," said the boy loudly.

"You better, if you know what's good for you," was the reply from outside the door. "Whoever's in there better hold himself easylike; there's a man at every window."

"There's nobody in here," called the boy. "What do you want?"

Brent smiled at the boy's attempt to protect him. "Better open up, son," he said softly. "Light the lamp first."

Alan struck a match and lighted the lamp. After a few moments of hesitation he went to the door and drew back the heavy bar.

Sheriff Ed Furness and two others pushed inside, holding their guns in readiness.

"Come out here, Brent!" cried the sheriff. "We saw the horse you stole in the corral, an' we know you're here. There's a bunch of men aroun' this cabin, an'—" He stopped speaking and brought his gun up as Brent stepped into the lighted room.

"Sheriff, couldn't you see fit to let a fellow get a little sleep?" complained Brent, rubbing his eyes.

"No man can sleep when I want him an' know where he is," replied the sheriff gruffly. "Maybe you've got one of those big words that'll fit this case," he added with a sneer.

"I sure have," said Brent with a grin. "It's *inopportune*—you know what that means? If you hang aroun' with me a while you'll get a regular vocabulary." He winked at Bill Lawton, who was one of the men with the official.

Ed Furness turned on the boy with a scowl. "Tryin' to harbor a criminal, eh? I guess you know that's against the law."

"I don't know much about law, an' I didn't know he was a criminal," said the boy stoutly.

"That's the stuff, son," said Brent cheerfully. "The sheriff don't know it either!"

"I know you stole a horse," said Furness grimly.

Brent looked at Bill Lawton in mock surprise. "Didn't you get your money for that hoss?" he asked.

"He had to give the money back to Lynch," said

the sheriff impatiently. "That makes it a matter of getting away with the horse. It won't do you any good to sling language, Brent; you're up against it."

Lawton was frowning at Brent. It was evident that he was puzzled.

"Can't you make me out?" Brent inquired easily. "Don't you know me?"

"I know you from seein' you this afternoon, you four-flusher," retorted Lawton. "That was raw stuff. You must be just startin' in."

"Now that ain't hardly right," said Brent plaintively. "You know I'm no four-flusher. Why don't you tell his nibs, here, who I am?"

"I don't know what you're tryin' to pull, but it's a fool stunt," said Lawton, his face darkening.

"Why, Bill?" Brent appeared crestfallen. "Didn't you lead 'em here? Ain't you goin' to claim the reward?"

"What—what—" Lawton's speech trailed off into muttered oaths as he stared at Brent under lowering brows.

"Go on, Bill, tell 'em," Brent urged.

"Go to blazes an' tell 'em yourself!" shouted Lawton, apparently at sea.

"Why, I thought everybody knew," said Brent with a wondering look. *"I'm Long Pete!"*

Lawton's jaw dropped and the sheriff tipped his derby back on his head with a snort while the boy cried out in astonishment. The faces of other members of the posse appeared in the doorway. The lamplight glinted on the barrels of many guns.

Then Steve Brent drew back his head and laughed loud and long.

CHAPTER FOUR

An Escape

"It won't do you any good to laugh, Brent," said Ed Furness slowly. "I wouldn't wonder if you was tall enough to be the man we're looking for at that. But you're not Long Pete. You can't bluff with me, an' I'm used to grins."

Brent stood smiling, rolling a brown-paper cigarette in his slim fingers. Lawton leaned on the table, a sneer on his lips.

"Aw, he ain't Long Pete!" cried the boy.

Lawton swung about. "Shut up, you brat!" The back of his left hand stung the boy's mouth.

Alan staggered back, the look of pained surprise on his face quickly changing to one of furious anger.

The cigarette had dropped from Brent's fingers with the slap. The smile froze on his lips. His eyes narrowed.

"Never mind him, sonny," he said; "he's just givin' us his pedigree."

"I'd give *you* more than that if you wasn't a prisoner of the law!" cried Lawton.

"What a fine hombre you'd be to work for," said Brent, arching his brows. "Maybe I'll take that job Lynch offered me yet!" He turned to Ed Furness. "Ed, I came out here with one hoss an' two hunches; now I reckon I ain't got any hoss, but I've got three hunches. I just got the hunch that if you want to release me, an' let me get my gun, which you notice I ain't wearin', or tell Bill, there, to put his away, I can make him crawl under that table!"

"That's enough," said Furness sharply. "I'm takin' you in, Brent." He motioned to the men at the door to mount, and they disappeared in the darkness. The other man with him and Lawton went out, leaving him, the Rabbit Foot foreman, Brent and the boy in the lighted room of the cabin.

The sheriff pointed a finger at Alan Carman. "I'm taking you in, too, to teach you a lesson," he said sternly.

"I don't care," said the boy defiantly.

"Oh, shucks! I don't reckon I'd take the boy in, Ed." It was Brent who spoke in a rather chilly tone. "I don't think it would make any better citizen out of him to have any such experience, do you, Sheriff?"

"It's time he was taught a lesson," said Furness. "Show 'em what they're up against an' it'll maybe stop 'em from going bad—if he hasn't gone bad already. Or maybe you told him to say you wasn't here, eh?"

"He didn't!" flared out the boy.

"An' he didn't know what he was doin' or why he was doin' it," said Brent, looking the sheriff steadily in the eye. "The boy just took a likin' to me an' I guess I let him think I was a shady character. A kid'll always stick up for the underdog, Ed."

"I'm not so sure that it looks what it is on the surface," snapped out Furness. "You an' him seem to know each other pretty well. Maybe you know old Frank Carman, too. I'm goin' to take the boy in an' question him."

"Why not do that here?" inquired Brent.

"We'll quit talking," said the sheriff, compressing his lips. "Get your hat an' coat, boy."

"An' I'll get mine," said Brent, turning swiftly and stepping into the darkened sleeping room.

It was done so suddenly and unexpectedly that Brent was in the other room before the sheriff could stop him. Furness had not been watching Brent as closely as he might because of the fact that Brent wore no gun.

The boy had preceded Brent into the other room.

"Watch out how you come out of there, Brent!" called the sheriff as he leaped to one side of the door while Lawton stepped quickly to the other side.

Brent's laugh floated out to them. "You must think I'm a fool, Ed, if you figure I don't know when I'm cornered. Besides, I sort of want to go back to town now anyway. I'm just feelin' around for my hat here, an' if you're scared of me making a break you can pot me when I step into the light."

While he was talking Brent secured his gun belt and hat. The boy held something cold against his hand, and Brent took it. It was another gun. Then the boy tugged at his sleeve, urging him to a corner of the small room. Brent threw the second gun out the door into the lighted room.

"If you're scared of me comin' out a-shootin', kick that gun under the table, Sheriff," he called out with another laugh.

He felt a cool draft of air strike his face and slipped to the corner of the room where he saw a dim square of light. He found a small door, and the boy just outside. He shut the door quickly, and they stole from the dense shadow by the cabin to the shed.

"They've took your horse aroun' front," the boy whispered. They were on the side of the shed away from the cabin.

"Listen," said Brent softly. "Do you know where you can hide aroun' here?"

"Sure, when we get in the woods," Alan replied.

"All right. You dig for the woods an' I'll draw their attention away. They'll take after me, but I figure on dodgin' 'em. No sense in you goin' in. Maybe I'll be back an' see you again, sonny."

"You got to come, too," the boy insisted. "There's horses back here a way," he added in an eager whisper. "Come on with me." His hand found Brent's.

Brent bit his lip in the darkness and pressed the hand. "You can't go with me, son. You'd only get into trouble an' there's no need of it—" He broke off as he heard the loud voice of Ed Furness in the cabin.

"Get aroun' to those windows, you fellows out there. I believe he's trying to beat it!"

They heard the pound of hoofs as the men again surrounded the cabin. Then:

"Brent, I'm coming in with the lamp! You haven't got a chance to get away, for my men have orders to shoot an' shoot straight. You can take a chance on me if you want to, for here I come!"

"There's nerve along with that derby hat," Brent muttered. "Come on, son, we'll scramble for the timber with the shed between us an' the cabin."

They heard Furness shouting in the cabin as they started for the dark shadow of the trees behind the corrals. The boy ran ahead along a path that led between the two empty corrals.

The shouts multiplied as the members of the posse called to each other. The escape of the pair had been discovered. Furness was roaring instructions to "get around the meadow" and not to shoot the boy.

They had almost reached the trees when shadows swept around the shed and shouts came from the horsemen who had discovered them.

"Run, son!" commanded Brent as he whipped out his gun.

There was a dart of flame from one of the rushing shadows and a bullet whined over their heads. Other riders turned toward them and the darkened space about the cabin was streaked with red as guns roared their warning.

Brent backed toward the trees and his own weapon spit fire. The nearest rider pulled his horse up short. Another rider swerved to the right, his mount crashed into the rails of the corral and sent the man spinning in the air.

Then Brent fell backward over some brush, turned swiftly and crawled into the shelter of the trees. As he stood up he felt the hand of the boy on his arm.

"Back this way," Alan cautioned, slipping his hand down until it met Brent's.

He dodged swiftly in among the trees which were too thick to permit a horse being ridden among them in the darkness. They came to a trail, and the boy led the way at a swift pace, whispering words of encouragement over his shoulder.

The shots ceased as the pursuers realized the futility of so spending their ammunition. The shouts died down, and Brent knew that Furness was holding a parley with his men. Brent knew also that while pursuit was impossible on horse-back in that wilderness, the sheriff would realize quickly enough that the fugitives could not expect to proceed far afoot.

It was safe to talk in an ordinary voice now, and he put a question. "Does Lawton know where the horses are back here—if there *are* any?"

"Nope," answered the boy. "We keep 'em in here where it'd be hard to find 'em. We don't want 'em stole. You ain't Long Pete, are you?"

Brent laughed softly. "Do you think I am, sonny?"

"Nope, I don't. Dad says a cow thief can't laugh natural, but you can."

"I'm afraid I've got you in a peck of trouble," said Brent in a worried voice. "An' we've made it all the worse by gettin' away an' you bein' along. Remember, if they catch us you'll have to agree to everything I say. I've got to take the blame, or it wouldn't be right, an' I've got to do what's right in this, Alan—do you understand?"

"Yes, I understand," replied the boy slowly. "Anyway, this is just fun for me, an' they couldn't put me in jail, could they?"

"I reckon they could," said Brent. "But they couldn't keep you there long," he added grimly.

"Pa says you've got to protect a man when he's your guest," the boy volunteered soberly.

"By Jupiter! Your dad has some regular-man ideas."

"I don't think he likes Bill Lawton any too much," said the boy; "an' me—I hate him!"

They were climbing a steep grade and now came out on the crest of the ridge. All sound of pursuit had ceased. The stars lighted the top of the ridge and Brent seized the opportunity to look at his watch. He exclaimed in surprise when he saw it was half past one in the morning.

"Only about three an' a half hours till daylight," he muttered.

"The horses are right down here," said the boy, leading the way down the other side of the ridge.

They came into a little meadow that was fenced. Brent saw several horses and watched in admiration as the boy caught one up and brought it to him.

"This is Hard Ribs, the best in the bunch," said Alan. "You can use him. There's a couple of saddles in that lean-to by the gate, an' you take the best—it's the biggest, anyway."

They bridled and saddled the horses and the boy rode ahead out of the meadow, along the base of the ridge to another trail.

"Which way you want to go?" he asked.

"Son, I want to hit the open country toward town—Rangeview."

"You goin' back there?" said the boy in surprise.

"Yep. I sure am. Just lead the way out, Alan, an' then I'll tell you something."

They started to the left on the trail in a direction which Brent concluded was east. Again he sang.

"It's hunches I'm playin', an' playin' em right;
I'm playin' em now on this ride in the night;

I'll be playin' em still when it comes daylight,
An' I'll bet that the hunches I'm playin' are right."

"How's that, sonny?" he asked with a light laugh.

"You made that up," the boy accused admiringly.

"I sure did," Brent agreed. "But I borrowed the tune."

They rode on in silence till finally they reached the edge of the sparse timber and Brent saw the shadowy plain ahead. He reined in his horse.

"Listen, sonny. Here's where we break company —for a time, anyway. I'm goin' into town, an' I've got to go alone. I'm borrowing this hoss, understand? An' if I can't get back right away I'll see that he's sent back. You tell your dad just what happened—the whole works, straight. An'—but where'll you go now?"

"I'd like to go along," said the boy wistfully, "but if you don't want me to—anyway, Pa ought to be back this mornin', an' I'll hang aroun' out of sight till he shows up. Lawton an' the others'll be combing the country hereabouts for you probably, an' they'll never think you'd go into town."

"That's the way I've got it figured," said Brent. "I'm bankin' on it, although that derby-hatted sheriff's no fool. But I've got to make the play. I'll be on my way now so's to make it by daylight. I know you can take care of yourself, sonny, an'— let's shake hands."

The boy brought his horse close, and Brent took his hand in a warm clasp.

"You got the makin's of a real man, Alan," he said soberly, "an' I'd hate to think I wouldn't see you again. So long."

"So long," called the boy.

When Brent was riding swiftly eastward on the prairie, Alan Carman turned about and rode straight back into the tumbled land the way they had come.

CHAPTER FIVE
Laird of the Range

Brent rode eastward for some time at a fast gallop—until the tumbled lands behind him were shrouded in deepest shadow and the morning mists, and he knew he could not be seen from that section. He entertained great respect for the courage and shrewdness of the sheriff who wore the derby.

"Ed Furness is no fool," he muttered; "not by a long shot. Well, c'mon, Hard Ribs, we'll drift down into town."

He turned into the southeast and slacked his pace, for his horse was lathered. After the manner of men who are much on the long trails alone, he spoke softly to himself, voiced his thoughts aloud to make his reasoning seem the more convincing.

"There's Furness; now he's on the square. An' he's dangerous. He means business. Lynch is the laird of the country—the biggest ranch owner, with his fingers on the county's finances through his bank. He's the big guy, an' he wants everybody to know it. I reckon I don't like him any too much for that reason. Bill Lawton's the bugaboo —Lynch's right-hand man in the cattle business. But he ain't above insultin' a stranger by makin' fun of his hoss, an' he ain't above slappin' a kid a quarter of his size an' less half his age. The kid's true blue. Sizes a stranger up, sees good in him, an' is ready to fight for him. Says he's got to protect a guest in his house. Dog-gone! His dad ought to be a good sort. An' they don't like Lawton an' Lawton don't like them. Some deal all around. An' nobody knows anything about Long Pete except he steals cattle in bunches an' leaves notes for receipts. An' everything named after rabbits! Some layout. Well, Steve, old boy, what say we copper a few bets!"

The eastern horizon took on a shade of gray and slowly brightened until its rim gleamed with the silver of the dawn. Brent saw the tall cottonwoods of Rangeview straight ahead and made for them at a canter. The sun was a disk of gold rising out of the eastern plain as he rode into the west end of town and around to the livery barn.

He found Jake, the barn man, already about. Jake stared at him with bulging eyes while Brent greeted him pleasantly.

"You will notice that I have still another hoss, Jake," he said amiably. "I am a man of many horses, it seems—an' many enemies. Did you look after Hunchy?"

"I did," gasped out the barn man. "He's in that stall there. I know you spotted him the minute you came in. What—how—"

"Well, if I saw any giraffes or not, it's a cinch I'm lookin' at a pup now," retorted the other thickly.

Brent reached over, took the man's glass, and spilled its contents on the floor. "When a man begins seein' *big* things an' thinks they're *small* things, he's had enough," he said coolly.

"You think you're big?" sneered his accoster. "I never seen a hoss thief yet that was very big."

Brent's eyes narrowed. "It's too early in the mornin' for trouble—with *you*," he said. "You better go get some sleep. You've wore out your welcome with us. Go call me names from the front or back door, but don't stand round so close."

"I'll—" The man's voice broke into a snarl, and he drew back to strike.

Brent caught his arm, whirled him about, and sent him spinning toward the rear door. The man lost his balance and fell on his left hand and knee. His right hand darted to the weapon at his side.

"Don't draw that gun!"

Brent's words rang on the stillness in a tone of unmistakable command. But the other's eyes were glowing red, and the hand on the butt of the gun snapped into action.

Jake leaped aside and the bartender ducked in a flash.

Brent's right hand shot downward, and the room echoed with the roar of his forty-five. The man on the floor dropped his weapon with a howl of rage and surprise. He scrambled to his feet and stood, shaking, staring at Brent. Blood dripped from the fingers of his gun hand. He was sobered, awed. The anger left his eyes.

"Maybe you better take that drink now," Brent invited with a nod to the bartender. "You're welcome."

The man advanced to the bar, took the drink the bartender put out for him in his left hand, and downed it in a single gulp.

"I didn't figure on hittin' your hand," said Brent, "but your gun was too close in against your side an' I just had to, I reckon."

The man looked at him, turned abruptly, picked up his gun in his left hand, and walked out the front door.

"Ain't nothin' serious," said Jake. "He started it, anyway. You're a tolerable shot, I'll say."

Brent raised his glass. "Who is he?" he asked, ignoring the compliment.

"Oh, that's Frank Carman from out Rabbit Butte way," was the answer.

Brent put down his glass. *"Who?"* he asked foolishly.

"Carman—Frank Carman," replied Jake, surprised at Brent's manner. "Why, you know of him?"

"Has he got a boy out there?" asked Brent.

"Yep. Right upstanding lad. Frank don't never

go home when he's the way he was this mornin'. Fact is, Frank's a sort of puzzle 'round here."

"Let's make it snappy," said Brent with a frown. "I've got business to tend to."

They took their drinks, and Brent paid the score, refusing to take another with Jake with the explanation that he was a "one-drink" man. They went out to the street and Brent left the barn man at the bank and walked back to the yellow house in which James Lynch lived.

He knocked at the front door. When it opened he stepped back and hastily removed his hat. In the doorway stood a girl. The rays of the morning sun, filtering through the leafy branches of the cottonwoods, struck golden gleams from her hair. Her cheeks glowed with the tints of rose petals, fresh with dew. Her full lips were red; her eyes were gray—questioning, but hinting of a cool confidence. Her figure would have driven a sculptor mad.

"I'm Carol Lynch," she said. "Whom do you wish to see?"

"Your—your—is he—your father?" stammered Brent.

"If you mean James Lynch, he is my uncle," replied the girl. "He is the only Lynch in town, except me. Do you wish to see him?" She smiled. Brent was not hard to look at as a specimen of the handsome male.

He nodded. "Yes, I'd like to see him."

As the girl turned there was a heavy step in the hall behind her. Then Lynch appeared, minus coat and collar.

"What are you doing back here?" he roared. "You got away from the sheriff, eh?"

"I was talkin' with the sheriff last night," said Brent, deliberately smiling at Carol Lynch. "I left him early this mornin' to come back to you an' report. I'd like to see you a few minutes."

"Oh, you would, eh? I suppose you'd like to have me take you over to my office so you could pull your gun on me an' go through the bank. Carol, go inside! You ain't got nothing in common with outlaws."

"Nor with gents she ain't acquainted with," said Brent pointedly. "I reckon she knows that without you tellin' her, Jim. But you better let her take my gun with her while we're talkin'. Maybe it'll ease your mind."

His right hand moved with incredible rapidity and he proffered the gun, butt first, on his open palm.

The girl's eyes cleared of doubt, and she took the gun. "Go see what he wants, uncle," she said sweetly. "If he *is* an outlaw, it's best I had his gun."

She retreated into the house with a ghost of a glance at Brent.

Lynch scowled, and then a grim smile hovered on his lips. "Brent," he said in a hard voice, "I'll give you credit for *one* thing: you certainly are a great actor."

"Better than you thought, Jim," said Brent quickly, "because I ain't actin'. Think that one over while we walk to the bank. I reckon the best place to talk business is in your office, after all."

Lynch hesitated. "Wait till I get my hat," he said and disappeared into the house. He returned shortly with his coat and hat on and Brent smiled as they started for the rear door of the bank.

"I see you're packin' it in your right coat pocket, Jim," he said cheerfully. "I should think a man like you would use a shoulder holster."

Lynch turned on him as he unlocked the door. "I couldn't hit a barn across the street," he said. "That weight in my pocket is a package of rare coins I had over to the house showing my niece. They're worth a lot of money." And he stood aside to allow Brent to enter.

When they were inside, Lynch led the way into his private office in the rear. He motioned Brent to a chair and sat down at his desk. He drew the package from his pocket and tossed it in a drawer.

"Now what do you think you want to see me about?" he asked, leaning on his elbows on the desk.

Brent took out tobacco and papers and began to fashion a cigarette. "I've been out toward the Rabbit Foot an' met your man Lawton for the second time," he said slowly. "I'll take that job, I reckon."

The banker leaned back in his chair and pursed his lips. But he didn't whistle. He broke into a short laugh. "It seems like I've got to keep on giving you credit," he said. "This time it's for nerve, pure an' simple. Just nerve!"

Brent touched a match to his cigarette, leaned toward Lynch, and looked him squarely in the eye. "Jim," he purred, "you haven't any idea how much nerve I've got!"

CHAPTER SIX
Saddle Logic

Lynch regarded the man across the desk from him with an awakened interest. He looked into the gray eyes that met his own fearlessly, noted the square chin, the clear, bronzed skin, the wavy brown hair above Brent's high brow. He frowned with a puzzled expression.

"Seems to me you could be in a better business than robbing banks," he observed. "A man that'll turn the trick you did, will do things worse than that."

"Was it robbin' you to borrow five hundred on security?" asked Brent mildly.

"Security!" exclaimed the banker. "You didn't leave any security."

"I left my hoss, Hunchy, an' I value him at about that sum—if I should think of sellin' him, I mean. You put a price on him yourself when you said you couldn't lend more'n five hundred on him."

"I was joking, an' you knew it," said Lynch angrily.

"I might have suspected it; but I didn't *know* it," replied Brent, smiling. "I always thought bankers didn't joke about loans. An' you wanted to do some business with me."

"It was getting money by force an' under false

pretenses," sputtered Lynch. "Just the same as robbery. The sheriff looked at it that way."

"No," said Brent, shaking his head. "The sheriff accused me of stealin' the black hoss. You say I robbed the bank. You two can't seem to agree on the charge."

"It's serious any way you look at it," declared Lynch.

"But there's no harm done," declared Brent. "The sheriff an' Lawton met up with me last night out north of the butte. Ed said Bill had given you back your five hundred, so you ain't out anything. Lawton got back his hoss so *he* ain't out anything. I've got my security back—so *I* ain't out anything. I can't see how a jury'd make much of a case out of this thing. Seems to me, the only man that's got a kick comin' is your clerk. *He* got scared an' got locked in the closet in the bargain."

Lynch looked about as if he had lost something. Then his gaze once more focused on Brent. "You're not bad," he said, stroking his chin. "It's refreshing to meet a clever talker like you once in a while."

"That ain't talk, it's logic—saddle logic," Brent pointed out with a gesture. "There's just one point that ain't satisfactory to me. My saddle is on Lawton's hoss."

"How come?" asked Lynch. "Why didn't you ask for it when the sheriff let you go?"

"I reckoned it would be on the hoss an' that

the hoss would be in the corral when I left where we was, but the hoss an' saddle an' bridle was gone."

Lynch looked at him shrewdly. "Does Ed know you're here?"

"I don't think so; but I wouldn't wonder if he did."

"What did you want that horse for when you had one, or something that looked like one, of your own?" demanded Lynch. "Oh, wait a minute—I know. You wanted a real good horse."

"No an' yes," drawled out Brent. "You see my hoss was dead tired, an' I wanted him to have a good rest. But I wanted to travel an' I needed a hoss for that. So you an' me an' Bill Lawton made our hoss deal."

"You didn't strike out like you thought it was any regular deal," said Lynch with a fierce glare. "You acted like you was going somewhere an' wanted to get there quick."

"I did," admitted Brent. "I was hittin' it fair an' good to try an' run across a gent's trail."

"Whose trail?" asked Lynch skeptically.

"Long Pete's trail," declared Brent. "You see the cards an' one thing an' another hasn't run any too free lately, an' I could use that two thousand reward—one thousand from *you,* an' one thousand from the county."

It was too much for Lynch. He banged a fist on his desk and swore. Then a crafty look came into his eyes. "I wonder if you *mean* that?" he exclaimed.

"Two thousand dollars' worth," said Brent.

"You know this Long Pete's been stealin' my cattle?" asked Lynch.

"I heard so, Jim—that's a fact, ain't it?"

"It is," grumbled the banker. "An' you want to go out on the Rabbit Foot to work because you think maybe you can get a clue to how Long Pete's working?"

"Exactly," Brent affirmed.

"Well, why didn't you do that in the first place? I offered you a regular job."

"Because Lawton made me sore, for one thing, an' I thought maybe I could do more if I sort of looked the ground over in my own way, for another."

"You have an answer for everything," said Lynch thoughtfully; "an' they seem to tie together."

"Another reason I didn't take the job yesterday was because you an' Ed tried to force it on me," said Brent.

"Now that sounds reasonable," mused Lynch. He wore a studied air. "What do you want to do out there?"

"Report to Lawton," said Brent shortly.

Lynch's eyes widened. "You an' Lawton got it in for each other?"

"It wouldn't be diplomatic for me to answer that

question, would it?" Brent countered. "Lawton's your foreman, an' I'm figurin' on goin' to work for you, under him."

Lynch rose and began to pace the room. Several times he stopped and looked at Brent. Finally he spoke in a tone of quick decision. "All right, you can go out there. I'll give you the fifty a month I first offered. Tell Lawton I said—"

"I'd rather you wrote it," Brent interrupted. "Just write a note sayin' you've hired me to work on the Rabbit Foot at fifty a month an' to take orders from Lawton. Date it this mornin' at nine o'clock. This means the hoss deal is all over, I take it."

"Oh, all right," said Lynch, sitting down at his desk. "Yes, the horse deal is all over—unless you try to pull something else." He wrote rapidly on a sheet of the bank's letter paper. He folded the message and handed it to Brent who read it, nodded, and put it in a pocket.

"I'll be goin' out directly," he said with a smile.

"I don't know exactly why I'm doing this, Brent," said Lynch with his usual frown; "but I'm taking a chance. I wish you luck. We'll go to the house an' I'll get your gun." He led the way out of the bank, locked the door, and they walked to the house.

"Maybe the young lady would prefer to return the gun herself," Brent suggested.

Lynch snorted. "Don't be a fool!" he said loudly as he went into the house.

But Brent had been right, for Carol Lynch appeared on the porch a few moments later with the weapon.

"I assumed you were no longer an outlaw when my uncle asked for this to return it to you," she said with a merry challenge in her voice.

"Your uncle has hired me to work for him on his ranch," said Brent. "You don't suppose he'd be hirin' an outlaw, do you?"

The girl looked doubtful. "What are you going to do out there?"

Brent shrugged. "Cow hands are not choosers of their tasks," he said, smiling.

"A pretty speech," approved the girl. But she looked at him keenly. "Have you ever killed anybody with that?" she asked, handing him the gun.

"If I had, ma'am, I sure an' certain wouldn't be boastin' of it to a lady," he replied, shoving the weapon in its holster.

"You are polite but evasive," she said, lifting her pretty brows.

Brent gazed at her in frank admiration. "It isn't hard to be polite to you, if that's what I'm doin'," he said.

"Maybe my uncle has hired you to teach his men manners," she said with a toss of her head. "I hope he hasn't hired you to kill anybody." She looked at him quickly.

"Carol, come in the house!" called her uncle.

"So long," said Brent with a flashing smile. "You better ask *him*." He walked rapidly to the street and met Frank Carman, who had his right hand bandaged.

"Hurt much?" he asked.

Carman eyed him malevolently. "What do you care?" he asked gruffly.

Brent frowned. "If I'd known it was you, I'd have found some other way," he said. "I didn't want any gun play with you."

"Oh, I ain't so fast with my gun," returned Carman sneeringly. "You don't need to run away from me. I ain't any faster when I'm out of likker than when I'm in it."

"Listen, Carman!" Brent spoke sharply. "Have you a hoss here with you?"

"Why—yes," said Carman.

"Then I want you to lead home a hoss I borrowed at your place last night. It's aroun' back of the barn. I'll have to keep your saddle an' bridle a while longer till I get back my own. You aimin' to start soon?"

"You was out to my place?" asked Carman, his gaze alert. "How did that happen?"

"Your boy will tell you all about it. Just you lead that hoss back. We'll get a halter an' rope at the barn, although you've probably got a rope. The boy's expectin' you this mornin'. I don't suppose you'd want him to know how we come to have trouble. You better be startin' back."

Something in Brent's tone caused Carman's eyes to glitter. Then, for a moment, they seemed frightened. "I was just goin'," he said finally.

"I'll walk down an' see you start," said Brent.

He went with Carman to the barn, saw him get his horse and saddle it. Then he unsaddled the other horse and took off the bridle. The barn man supplied a halter and Carman attached his own rope. Without a word to the barn man or Brent, Carman rode away toward the west.

Brent put the saddle and bridle Alan Carman had loaned him on his own horse Hunchy. "Seems to be in pretty fair shape, at that," he commented to Jake.

"He's all right," answered the barn man, grinning. "There's more horse there than the rest of 'em think."

"Well, don't try an' wise 'em up, Jake," said Brent with a wink.

"I ain't tryin' to edgycate anybody," was the reply.

"I'll be back in a few minutes," said Brent. "I'll leave Hunchy tied to the corral."

He went around to the hotel and entered the dining room. "Ham an' eggs," he ordered tersely. His brow was furrowed in thought as he waited for his breakfast.

"Old coins," he muttered to himself. "Old coins an' worth a lot of money. An' I thought he had a gun. He wasn't scared of me, at that. He's no fool, either. Both of 'em smart—Ed and Jim. Now what about Lawton?"

He was lost in thought as he ate his breakfast. He paid for it and walked to the barn, still thinking. The barn man untied his horse and handed him the reins. When Brent was in the saddle he leaned toward Jake and spoke.

"What do you know about Long Pete, Jake?"

"As much as you do—if that's little enough," was the ready reply.

"Does any of his gang ever hit town?"

"Not as anybody knows of," informed the barn man. "How long has he been workin' his game aroun' here?"

"Just last fall an' this spring. There's some big rewards out."

"I know," Brent said with a nod. "I was wonderin' if anybody knew what he looks like."

Jake shook his head. "I reckon not; but Jim Lynch has some specimens of his handwritin' that he left for Lawton thankin' him for the cattle he made off with."

"Then he's what you'd call a polite rustler," answered Brent laughingly as he rode off with a wave of farewell.

He struck westward across the prairie and almost immediately began to whistle cheerfully. Coming at a furious pace toward town were a number of horsemen. Brent burst forth in song.

"The cat found the rat hole an' hung aroun'
   all night;
But the rat went out another hole an' never
   came in sight.
So the rat watched the cat while the cat
   watched in vain,
An' finally the two of them got caught in the
   rain."

He laughed boisterously at his own composi-
tion. But his eyes were hard and cold as he
leaned forward in the saddle and patted his horse
on the neck.

CHAPTER SEVEN

Hunchy Performs

The approaching riders came on apace and Brent grinned with the reflection that they were not riding so fast because of his presence on the plain, because they could not possibly have made him out at that distance, but because Ed Furness must have arrived at the conclusion that he, Brent, had gone on into town. He had rather expected the sheriff to so decide; for he did not underrate the official's ability.

He jogged on, singing his new song with quaint variations in the text; but as the riders drew near and he saw by their gestures and shouts that he had been recognized, he swerved to the right and reined in his horse.

Ed Furness was in the lead when they rode up, and his gun was in his hand. He stopped close to Brent, turned in his saddle, and spoke.

"So you lied to me, eh? You told me he'd gone north when he went east." He turned and looked at Brent savagely. But Brent disregarded him and smiled at the boy on a horse behind him with the other five members of the posse. Lawton wasn't with them.

"I reckon you thought I *was* goin' north, sonny,

an' I don't blame you, the way I acted," he said as the boy flushed.

"You can't put that over, Brent," said the sheriff sharply. "The boy rode into the meadow before daylight an' told us you'd gone north. Either he was trying to throw us off the track on his own hook, or he was following your orders."

"Then you can believe he was followin' my orders, Ed," said Brent coldly. "You seem powerful anxious to take somebody into town, even if it's only a boy."

"I'll take both of you now," said the sheriff, scowling. "You had a poor hunch this time if you thought you could get to town, grab your own horse, an' beat it to the mountains this way while we were hunting you up north."

"I wasn't hittin' for the mountains, Sheriff," said Brent, leaning on his saddle horn and regarding the official gravely. "I'm hittin' for the Rabbit Foot Ranch to go to work."

"Not bad—not bad at all," said Furness with a glimmer of admiration in his eyes. "I suppose you think Lawton would be scared to take you on. An'—you might have been easing back this way thinking to get your saddle," he added as a startling after-thought.

"I aim to do that, too," said Brent. "An' I expect Lawton will take me on. He's workin' for Jim Lynch, ain't he? An' Jim Lynch gave me a job."

"We're losing time here," said Furness with a significant look at his men.

"You sure are, Sheriff," said Brent. "Take a look at that." He drew out the note Lynch had written and passed it to Furness.

Furness read it, studied it, and became thoughtful. "You went in there to see Lynch?" he asked.

"I sure did, an' had the good luck to meet Miss Carol, too. Jim understands why I didn't take the job first time he offered it to me yesterday. He says the hoss deal is all over an' nobody hurt. He gave me a job on the ranch an' he realizes there's nothing to prosecute about. I'll take that note back. I've got to give it to Lawton."

Furness handed back the note, pushed his derby back on his head, and surveyed Brent with a queer smile. "There's one man in this country that I know a lot about an' can't lay a finger on," he said slowly, as if measuring his words; "but I can lay a finger on you an' I don't know much of anything about you. When a man has me guessing I don't mind telling him so to his face. But I'd bet you've got no idea of goin' to work on the Rabbit Foot."

"Well, Sheriff," said Brent, returning the smile, "you can't very well spare the time to go out there an' watch me work, but that's just what I aim to do. An' I reckon there's something you've overlooked. I could have gone north; an' I could have gone east or south out of Rangeview this mornin' instead of comin' back on this way. As for the saddle—if I'm an outlaw like I think *you* think, I could have picked up a saddle most any place."

"You couldn't have got far on that horse," declared Furness.

"No? Watch this!"

Before the sheriff or any of the men with him realized his intention, Brent shook out his reins and drove in his spurs. Hunchy lurched ahead, swept past them in mighty bounds, and was running west of them.

Furness shouted and gave chase, the others following him, except the boy, Alan, who sat his horse and watched the unique exhibition— temporarily forgotten.

The sheriff evidently concluded it was a trick, for he pushed his horse to its utmost in pursuit of Brent. He even fired several shots, but aimed wide and shook his head at his men. He did not want to drop Brent, for if it was true that Lynch had hired him, and would not prefer charges, Brent was not a fugitive from the law.

Brent rode west for a distance, then cut south. Hunchy easily kept his lead while the sheriff swore and wondered. Then Brent edged around to the east again and Hunchy flew past them for the second time in an even greater burst of speed. Now Brent rode straight for the boy, Alan, sitting his horse and marveling at the spectacle. When he reached him he shouted to the boy to get up behind him. Alan obeyed, his eyes shining with eagerness, and then they were off, barely twenty feet ahead of Furness and his men, with Hunchy carrying a double load.

They rode north, and if the sorry-looking horse had shown speed before, he now displayed an ability to all but fly. The sheriff, mounted on an excellent horse, left his men behind in the pursuit, striving his best to overtake Brent and the boy. But Brent's horse steadily increased his lead. It seemed to Sheriff Furness, swearing and marveling and losing ground fast, that Hunchy was all legs and neck and that his feet never touched the ground. He had never witnessed such speed in a horse. Nor did Hunchy seem to tire, although the sheriff's horse was showing the effects of the strain; he was slowing. Furness swore now in admiration. Hunchy was so far in the lead that he couldn't hope to overtake him, although he had outdistanced his own men. And if anything, Hunchy was increasing his pace!

The sheriff checked his mount in acknowledgment of defeat. Then Brent turned about and came racing back. As he brought Hunchy to a rearing stop he covered Furness with his gun. The sheriff had been so amazed at the performance that he had had no thought of the weapon he had returned to his holster. His men were far behind and coming slowly.

· · ·

"Two convincers!" said Brent evenly. "I've got the drop on you, Ed, like I could have had it once or twice before, if you only knew it. An' I've shown you that I could have got away if I wanted to. Also, Jim Lynch had pretty good security in this hoss if he'd only known it. Now, Ed, I don't give a hang if we get along or not, but I want you to lay off this kid. Whatever the play is, he ain't in on it. I reckon you can see I'm tellin' you the truth. Does he go home or doesn't he? Hurry up an' talk, Ed, for I ain't goin' to wait till your crowd gets here."

"He goes," said Furness, his eyes narrowed to slits.

"Get down, Alan," Brent ordered. Then as the boy slipped to the ground: "The sheriff'll have one of the men bring you your hoss. Then you hit for home. I 'spect your dad's there by now."

Furness's men were nearly up to them. Brent thrust his gun back in its holster.

"Now, I'm goin' on to the ranch an' report," said Brent coolly.

The sheriff made no reply, nor did he attempt to draw his weapon.

Brent wheeled his horse and struck west toward Rabbit Butte. Looking back, he saw the sheriff's men join him. They sat their horses for a spell and then turned toward town. Brent smiled.

"But he ain't satisfied," he thought to himself.

"Furness is smart an' he's takin' no chances. He'll talk with Lynch first thing an' maybe convince him he's wrong in takin' me on. Then he'll come bustin' out here with blood in his eye. I've got to move fast if I'm goin' to play my hunches."

His thoughts were interrupted by a sight that held his gaze for several minutes. There were cattle north of the butte. He had understood from the boy that the Rabbit Foot did not range stock north of the butte. True, this herd was not far north —not as far as the rough country—but they were a long way from the cattle grazing to southward.

"Looks like prime stuff, too," Brent muttered. "Reckon I'll look aroun' a bit before I report."

He turned north and jogged along, leaning forward, bent in the saddle, looking exactly like a rider who was making his way home, half asleep. The ranch and the butte were a considerable distance away. He gained the screen of a bunch of willows growing in some marshy ground and stopped.

Looking toward town Brent saw a rider proceeding west, leading a horse.

"He's keepin' his word to the kid," said Brent to himself. "I knew I could trust him to do that."

He could not make out the boy because he was probably sitting on the ground, waiting for his horse. Then he looked toward the butte again, whistled in surprise, and rubbed his eyes. The small herd of cattle north of the butte had disappeared!

CHAPTER EIGHT
Swift Turns

Brent puzzled over the disappearance of the cattle for a few minutes and then laughed to himself.

"Steve, you're a plumb fool—you're loco," he said aloud. "Now you scc a bunch of cattle an' now you don't. Do you reckon they was rustled or something right under your eyes? Didn't the boy say there was a fence along here between the rough ground an' the north end of the butte? He did. Do you think they jumped the fence? They didn't. Is there a break in the fence? There might be. But it's a better bet that they was drivin' that bunch over to the range west of the butte."

After this soliloquy he thought rapidly for several minutes.

"I reckon it wouldn't do any harm to look that ground over north of the butte," he concluded, again speaking aloud. "But it ain't noon yet an' it might be better to wait till long in the afternoon."

Brent dismounted to wait. He rubbed Hunchy's nose and complimented him on the morning's performance. "You're sure worth five hundred of *any*body's money, old hoss," he declared in the dun's ear; "an' I wouldn't sell you for twice that much!"

He rolled a cigarette and smoked while the boy

came at a gallop. When the youth was nearly opposite him to eastward, Brent mounted and rode out to join him.

Alan Carman's face lit up with genuine joy and admiration when he saw him.

"Well, you're a nice kid," he finally blurted out, "an' I ain't had many trustin' friends lately, an' that's a fact. I kind of got on the off trail, son. An' that's what you've got to be careful about. The time to keep out of messes, Alan, is when you're young. If you can steer clear of trouble when you're young you're pretty apt to be able to steer clear of it right on through. But that doesn't mean you should let anybody hang anything on you. Stick up for your rights an'—oh, I reckon I'm gettin' in too deep. How far is it to your place?"

"Only about five miles from here," replied the boy.

"Well, if you've got enough in the cabin to eat, I'll jog along with you an' have dinner," said Brent, grinning.

"There's lots to eat," Alan declared. "Thought you was goin' to work on the Rabbit Foot."

"I am," replied Brent. "But I can report in the afternoon just as well as now an' be more likely to find Lawton there. He's probably out on the range this time of day."

"No he ain't," said the boy. "He took some men an' started north this mornin'. The sheriff kept me with him while they hunted aroun' our place an' to the west. Then he got the idea suddenlike that you'd gone into town. Lawton said he'd bet a thousand dollars you was one of Long Pete's gang, an' if they could catch you again they could probably use you to round up Long Pete an' the others."

"Oh, that was Lawton's idea, eh?" Brent said, half to himself. "How long has Lawton been the foreman out here?"

"Five years," the boy answered. "He's done quite a lot. Got Jim Lynch to put in better cattle, thoroughbreds; hired men as knew all about handling such cattle. He says it was puttin' in the good cattle that brought the cow thieves here last fall."

"Did he put the good stuff in the first year he was here?" asked Brent.

"Second year," said the boy. "It took him a year to talk old Lynch into it."

Brent drew his right foot out of the stirrup and swung it idly. "Well, let's see. He must have had his first lot of good beeves last fall, then."

"Sure did," confirmed the boy. "An' as soon as they were ready to ship they began stealin' them. They lost a hundred an' fifty head last fall an' a hundred head this spring, or something like that."

The boy talked eagerly, sincerely, willingly. It was plain he was glad to tell Brent everything he could; that he trusted him and liked him.

"How do you an' your dad get along?" Brent asked suddenly.

"Fine," replied the boy. "He's good to me. Oh, once in awhile—" and his young face clouded for an instant but brightened immediately.

"Yes," prompted Brent; "once in awhile . . ."

"He comes home feelin' kinda bad from town," admitted the boy. "But all the men do that, don't they? I heard they did."

"Yes, most of 'em do," Brent agreed. "There's another thing, son. You want to be careful of towns. Treat 'em like you would a good horse an' they'll be good to you; but try to *ride 'em* an' they'll buck an' throw you. Know what I mean? Don't be too hard with the spurs."

The boy laughed with delight. "I know what you mean," he said. "You mean to stay away from the rough houses."

"You said it," returned Brent, pleased. "But I ain't no preacher."

They turned into the trail that led into the tumbled country north of the butte where the Carman cabin was located. It was the same trail by which Brent had left after midnight. As before, the boy rode ahead. When they came to the corral, Alan cried out.

"Why, there's the horse I let you take. I didn't ask about it because I thought you left it in town."

"An' I didn't mention it because I sent him back with your dad," said Brent, nettled that he was compelled to disclose the fact that he had met the elder Carman in town.

"Oh, you met Pa?" asked Alan, his face brightening.

"Just for a minute," said Brent. "We better ride right on to the cabin, don't you think?"

"Sure. Must be Pa is there."

But when they reached the meadow where the cabin was located they failed to see Carman's horse in the corral. The boy seemed disappointed, but said nothing as they dismounted, unsaddled, and looked after their horses. They found the cabin empty.

"Guess he rode down to the ranch," the boy decided. "I'll get us some dinner."

"An' I'll help," Brent offered.

But the boy would not accept his assistance. So Brent went out into the meadow and looked around. He crossed to the west side and found a trail which ran through that side of the meadow north and south.

"Must be the trail I came in on last night," he muttered. He found the tracks of horses that had gone north, and there was one fresh track leading south.

"I reckon the kid's right," he thought to himself. "Old Carman's gone down to the ranch."

He went back to the cabin and in a short time dinner was ready. After they had eaten, Brent confessed that he could do with an hour or two of sleep. He did not wish to go down toward the ranch until late in the afternoon, for he wanted to look the ground over at a time when he thought there would be no one north of the butte.

He sought the bunk he had occupied for a time the night before and was soon asleep. He was awakened by the boy shaking him gently.

"You've been asleep more'n three hours," said Alan. "It's after three o'clock."

"Then I'll be on my way," said Brent, getting up. "Your dad home yet?"

The boy shook his head. "He's gone down to the ranch, I guess. He'll be home by supper time, though."

Brent bridled and saddled his horse and asked the boy about the trail south. He learned that the trail leading through the west side of the meadow led south, but that there was a trail turning off from it about three miles down that led to a gate in the fence directly north of the butte. He thanked the boy, promised to come to see him again, and started down the trail.

Brent hurriedly descended the slope of the ridge to the main trail and galloped southward. When he thought he had covered half the distance to the edge of the bad lands he turned off the trail behind a screen of cedar bushes.

In a few minutes he heard the ring of hoofs on the trail below him and a rider came into sight, pulling up his horse against the grade. Brent recognized Carman. It had been he who had been arguing with the horseman at the edge of the rough country. It did not take Brent long to make up his mind. He waited until Carman had nearly gained the top of the grade and then rode out from the shelter of the bushes and trees and blocked his way in the trail.

Carman recognized him with an inarticulate cry that sounded like a snarl.

"Hello, Carman," he greeted, as if he hadn't noticed the other's displeasure at sight of him. "Been home yet?"

Carman's manner suddenly underwent a striking change. Suspicion shone in his eyes. His manner lost its aggressiveness. He became almost meek.

"Yes, I was home," he said mildly. "Left the horse an' rode down to the Rabbit Foot to see if I could get a job for the rest of the summer."

"I'm lookin' for the same thing," said Brent with a smile. "Did you have any luck?"

"No," replied Carman shortly. "They're not takin' on any men. Guess you'll have to go south of Rangeview if you want work. You can make town by a little after dark an' get down there in the mornin'. Lots of good outfits down there."

His effort to direct him away from the Rabbit Foot was not lost on Brent. "Who is the boss down below?" he asked.

"Cow boss is Nagel," said Carman with a slight frown. "Won't do you no good to see him."

"Did you see him?" Brent inquired.

"Yes," replied Carman uneasily. "Turned me down flat. Why don't you hit south? I would, but I live up here."

Brent edged his horse closer to Carman's and looked at him steadily. "Ain't Lawton the big gun down there?" he asked.

"If you knew it, why'd you ask me?" flared out Carman. "You've got a funny way of talkin' an' actin'. What are you? An association man?"

"I never worked for a cattlemen's association in my life," said Brent. "I'm lookin' for somebody."

The uneasy manner returned. "Who you lookin' for?" asked Carman.

"I'm lookin' for Long Pete!" said Brent, leaning forward in the saddle.

He saw Carman start. The man looked at him quickly in a wild way. He looked aside an instant later and wet his lips. He gave Brent the impression that he was afraid of him, or, he might be terrorized at mention of the rustler's name.

"What you want him for?" he managed to ask.

"I want to give him a message."

Carman shifted in his saddle. His gaze, when he again looked at Brent, was puzzled.

"Who from?" he asked with a crafty glint in his eyes.

Brent's brows went up. "I reckon I can't tell you that," he replied coldly. He couldn't decide whether it was cunning or understanding that gleamed in Carman's eyes.

"You know where my place is, an' how to get there?" asked Carman. "You said you'd been there an' seen my boy."

"I know where it is," Brent said with a nod.

"You be there at midnight," said Carman.

"That's straight goods, Carman?" said Brent soberly.

Carman shrugged. "I said it."

"I'll be there," said Brent, turning out of the trail so the other could pass.

He sat his horse quietly for some minutes, staring after the man until he had disappeared around a turn in the trail.

"Now, dang it!" he muttered. "I wanted to see what effect the name would have on him an' look what I stepped into. Hunchy, this is sure gettin' interestin'. An' I can't make that hombre out. Well, anyway, I've got time to size up the ranch an' beat it back."

He rode down the trail and in a short time came to the gate. It was plain from the condition of the trail that no cattle were moved through the gate. He passed through and rode west along the fence. He continued for two miles, but could see no sign where any considerable number of cattle had been driven in that direction, nor were there any evidences that there had been any breaks in the fence.

"Maybe Long Pete just naturally drives 'em south," he thought. "Why not? But where this bunch went to that was up here to-day's got me."

It was sunset and he turned back. He rode within a quarter of a mile of the gate, so as to fix its exact location in his mind, and then turned south, directly toward the butte. He looked closely at the grass, but could not determine whether there had been much grazing there or not.

When he reached the rolling slopes that formed the lower part of the north side of the high butte he turned westward. It was a flat country around the butte, and he estimated it was fully fifteen miles around the four sides. The butte itself was a miniature mountain on the plain.

The twilight was falling, veiling the land in blue and purple mists, as he turned along the west side of the butte. Then he heard the echoes of flying hoofs. He looked behind and saw two riders dashing around the north side toward him. He hesitated, in doubt as to whether to wait and meet them or make away. Then he remembered Carman's advice to be at his place at midnight. If he should wait for the two horsemen he might be delayed for some reason and fail to keep the appointment at Carman's. He decided to avoid the two oncoming riders, and even as he arrived at the decision, he wondered which way they had come from.

He tickled Hunchy with his spurs and the dun

broke into a gallop. At that instant there were two streaks of red in the dusk and two guns barked.

Brcnt turned west, letting Hunchy out. The pursuers cut west also. As they were north of Brent, the direction in which they wanted to go, he had to pass them. He pushed his horse, edging northwest, with the pair of riders coming for him at a tangent. There were more shots, and lead whistled past his ears.

Brent's eyes flashed. He saw that they might be able to cut him off from the gate even if he made the edge of the timber on the west slope; for he would have to turn back. A bullet nearly tore the hat from his head.

"That means business!" he cried aloud, and turned his horse on a straight line for the gate.

One of the men was closer to him than the other and this man rode directly at him, his gun blazing.

Brent drew his weapon, turned his horse slightly to the left, rose in the stirrups, and fired.

The approaching rider leaned far to the right in his saddle while his horse reared. Then he tumbled, and his horse lunged forward dragging him with a foot in the stirrup.

Brent turned and raced toward the horse's head. The other rider was coming up and firing. The stricken man's foot came loose from the stirrup and he lay motionless on the ground while the horse dashed away.

Bullets were flying again and Brent once more struck for the gate. He found the man who was following was mounted on the best horse ridden by any man he had met that day. For a moment he wondered if the pair could be members of the band of rustlers. He spurred Hunchy and gained. The man behind had quit firing. Then Brent approached the fence and the gate.

"Here's where we show 'em something, hoss!"

He kept his spurs against the horse's flanks and the animal sailed over the fence and gate, struck the hard trail on the other side, and plunged into the shadow of the trees.

CHAPTER NINE
Man to Man

In the shadows Brent drew his mount up sharply. He listened and heard the dull echoes of hoofs retreating across the plain. The rider who had followed him was going back to the aid of his injured companion; perhaps he would find him dead. Brent shrugged. He had wanted no trouble of the kind, but he had no alternative. He had fled from the second man to avoid the necessity of shooting him. He was lucky, indeed, that he hadn't been shot himself.

He considered two phases of the situation for a few moments. If he had waited for them and they had proved to be Rabbit Foot men, he would have had no trouble in establishing his right to be on that range. But he could not have avoided going back to the ranch with them, a thing he did not wish to do. He had no intention of not being at Carman's cabin at midnight.

And so he came to the meadow and saw a light in Carman's cabin window. He dismounted and led his horse off the trail. Hunchy had been well fed that noon and had grazed until nearly four o'clock on the rich grass of the meadow. Therefore he was in good shape. Brent tied him to a tree and loosened the cinch of the saddle. Then he rolled a cigarette, lighted it in the shelter of the trees and bushes and, keeping its glowing end cupped in his palm, went back to where he had a good view of the meadow and the cabin. He sat down to wait.

There was no movement about the cabin; nor could Brent see any horses in the corrals behind the shed. After a time he became uneasy and decided to investigate. He rose and walked slowly in the shelter of the trees to the east side of the meadow. Then he proceeded north until he was close to the corrals behind the shed and cabin. He had ascertained that the cabin door was closed. Light shone in both windows of the larger of the two rooms.

He waited again for a spell near the corrals and then stole softly to the shed. He looked in and found there were no horses there. The cabin windows were open, but he could hear no sound from within. He made his way cautiously to one of the windows and peered in. The boy, Alan, was sitting by the table, asleep in his chair. There was no one else in the room.

Brent stepped back with a frown and looked quickly around. Carman had left the cabin. Still it was to be expected, he reflected. If the man was in earnest when he intimated that someone would be there to meet Brent, he would naturally have to go for him. Brent was undecided, but finally he went around to the door and let himself in.

He woke the boy, who jumped up with a start and threw up his hands as if to ward off a blow. When he recognized Brent he dropped them, looked foolish, and then smiled.

Brent wondered if someone had struck the boy—his father, perhaps. "Where's your dad?" he asked.

"Dunno. He went out soon's he had supper an' rode away." The boy's tone was worried, and there was a glimmer of doubt in his eyes.

Brent sat down. "What's the matter, son? Didn't your dad like it because I'd been here?"

The boy smiled again, apparently reassured. "Guess he didn't," he confessed. "Reckon he heard how we sort of traveled together last night, an' he gave me the dickens."

"Was he—rough?" asked Brent.

"No—no," stammered the boy loyally, although Brent could see he had hit the mark.

"Looks like the two of us is bound to be tied together in trouble, sonny," said Brent, patting the boy on the knee. "But I reckon we'll pull out. I'm goin' to get out of here because I don't want anybody to come along an' find us here chinnin'. I wouldn't care so far's *I* was concerned, but you've got to stay outside this business from now on."

"You had your supper?" asked Alan.

"I sure have," lied Brent cheerfully. "I was expectin' somebody to show up here, maybe, an' later I want to see your dad. But if anybody comes before I show up, just forget I was here—mind."

The boy nodded with another smile as Brent slipped to the door. But Brent didn't go out at once. He stood frowning for a moment, then his brow cleared. "You don't have to forget I was here, son," he said slowly. "You just needn't *say* I was here unless your dad or somebody asks you. Then tell 'em the truth." He went out the door.

Before he could reach the shed he heard horses galloping into the meadow from the south trail. There was no time to make the shadow of the trees. The riders were coming at a gallop—two of them. Brent ran behind the cabin into the shed which was a three-sided affair, open on the side toward the cabin.

He was hardly in the shadow when the horsemen rode up to the first corral and dismounted. He leaned out in an effort to catch a glimpse of the men, and a weight hit him, throwing him to the ground with a force which nearly knocked the wind out of him. An arm twisted around his neck.

"I've got him!" his assailant cried in hoarse satisfaction.

Brent recognized Bill Lawton's voice. He hunched his back in a tremendous effort and literally doubled under, breaking Lawton's hold around his neck and partly throwing him off. This gave him a momentary advantage, and he was quick to avail himself of it. He jerked free of Lawton's right arm and brought his left elbow up with all his strength. It struck Lawton on the jaw, and the Rabbit Foot foreman grunted. Then Brent came clear and leaped to his feet just as Lawton's companion rushed to his aid. It was Carman, and Brent planted his right square on the point of the man's chin. Carman went down like a log.

"Turn aroun' an' march to the door of the cabin," said Brent sternly. "You, too, Carman—I'm watching you."

Carman raised his hands of his own accord and the pair walked to the front of the cabin.

"Wait a minute!" Brent commanded. "I reckon I better go ahead."

He stepped past them, backed into the cabin, and ordered them to follow. He kept them covered as they entered.

"Was this the gentleman who was to lead me to Long Pete, or take the message?" he asked Carman.

Carman appeared too befuddled to talk.

"If anybody knows anything about Pete, you're that hombre," said Lawton with a black look.

"So that's it," said Brent smilingly. "Carman thought he better report the matter of my little request to headquarters, eh? An' have me here so you could pick me up. Well, Lawton, you ain't overburdened with brains. Funny you got back from the north so quick."

Lawton glared. "Go ahead. Get to the point, whatever it is."

"It ain't a point," said Brent in a smooth voice; "it ain't a point, Lawton, it's a letter." He drew the note Lynch had written from a pocket and held it out to the Rabbit Foot foreman.

"Take it with your left hand an' read it, Lawton; but don't get careless with your right."

Lawton took the note as directed and scanned it. A look of stupefaction showed on his face. He stared at Brent in bewilderment. Then his eyes blazed.

"I had you pegged as a four-flusher from the start!"

Brent's eyes narrowed, and he pressed his lips into a white line.

"I believe you poked a gun in Lynch's ribs an' made him write that," said Lawton with a sneer.

"That might have happened," Brent agreed.

Lawton was nettled at this retort. "What do you want of me?" he asked darkly.

"Nothin' much—if you think that letter's a fake or was forced," Brent said coolly.

"You're playin' a crafty game," said Lawton. "You didn't come here just to make trouble. You've been movin' aroun' quite regular. Callin' yourself Long Pete!" He sneered again. "An' wantin' to send a message to him. I wouldn't be surprised if while you've drew me up here the rest of your gang was workin' at my stock!"

"That could be," Brent admitted.

"You've called yourself what you are, you—you—cow thief."

"Lawton, you can drop your right hand!"

Brent slipped his gun in its sheath.

The letter fluttered to the floor. For a space of several seconds the men looked into each other's eyes as Lawton's hand came slowly down. It hung at his belt line for an instant, then flashed into action as Brent dropped to the left, whipped out his weapon, and fired twice before Lawton could complete his draw. There was a crash of glass and the room was plunged in darkness as Lawton's gun roared.

Brent had fired at the lamp!

Again Lawton's gun roared, and again—until it was empty. Then silence. After a time there was a rasping sound and a match flared into flame. Lawton peered about in the faint light.

"Get another lamp," he commanded hoarsely.

The match went out. Someone was moving. Lawton struck another match, and the boy came with a new lamp. Lawton touched the wick with a burning match and when it lighted, he looked around. The curses streamed from his lips.

Brent was gone.

CHAPTER TEN

A Forced Hand

At nine o'clock next morning Steve Brent sauntered into the little office of Sheriff Ed Furness in the brick jail in Rangeview.

Furness was at his flat-topped desk, and when he saw who his visitor was he sat back in his chair, tipped his derby over his eyes, and thrust his thumbs into the armholes of his vest.

"Good mornin', Ed," said Steve Brent.

"Did you come in to give yourself up?" asked the sheriff pleasantly.

"I thought you was goin' to say give myself away, Sheriff," answered Brent.

"You've already done that," declared Furness, tipping back his derby.

"So?" Brent looked surprised. "I thought I was playin' my hand sort of neat."

"You was—till you failed to show up at the Rabbit Foot yesterday noon," said the sheriff.

"How news travels in this country," Brent complained. "That must be why everything's named after rabbits. Everything is on the hop, skip, an' jump."

"Including you," the sheriff added. "Where from this morning?"

"I've had a deplorable—there's a good word, Ed—a deplorable experience," said Brent in sorrowful tones. "I had to spend most of the night on top of a high ridge in that bad-land country north of the butte."

"Watching for smoke signals from Long Pete, I suppose," said Furness with a wry smile.

"Well, I might have seen a signal, at that," replied Brent. "An' then I might have imagined it. I've got a good imagination, Ed."

"You have," Furness agreed. "Almost too good. I sometimes think you're a little cracked."

"It would look that way from the way I've flirted with you, Ed; but then, it ain't every man in this country that knows how to handle you."

"What's *that?*" exclaimed Furness, bringing his feet down off the rungs of his chair.

"No offense, your worship," said Brent with a wave of the hand. "Just an idle thought."

"No, it ain't an idle thought!" thundered the sheriff, slamming the desk with his fist. "You're playin' me for a sucker!"

"I'm glad you see finally that there's something serious in this," said Brent coolly.

"I'm goin' to lock you up," said Furness with determination, "till I can get your pedigree."

"I'm wearin' it on the right-hand side, mister," said Brent in a hard voice, "an' I'm ready to save you the trouble of goin' to Texas or blazes to find out about me any time!"

94

"Oh, you're coming clean," said Furness, his eyes narrowing.

"Call it that if you want to," was Brent's retort; "but I'm here on business an' the pleasantries are all over, so far's I'm concerned."

The sheriff smiled. "I'm givin' you plenty of rope," he hinted.

"An' I'm goin' to start takin' up the slack," said Brent. "The hoss deal ain't over as I look at it. You're the sheriff of this county. I want you to go out to the Rabbit Foot an' get my saddle an' bridle that was on the black hoss when Lawton took him back."

"You what?" exclaimed Furness with a gasp.

"Now you're not hard on hearin'," said Brent impatiently. "I want the saddle. I can't go near that ranch without some of those hombres out there opening up on me with their six-guns. They must need practice or else they reckon I'm a natural target. I didn't think Lawton would be there at noon yesterday, an' I drifted up to the Carman place with the kid for dinner. I had another reason for that move that I ain't explainin' right now. I met Lawton later, an' he laughed at Jim's note an' the guns came out. I passed him up. He's still breathin' the good old prairie air. If he's got any sense, he'll probably ride in to-day to find out if the note was O. K. But I ain't waitin' for that. I'm goin' out there an' get my property, the first thing. All I'm askin' *you,* Sheriff, is, do you want me to go alone?"

Ed Furness showed by his manner that the pleasantries also were all over with him. He looked into Brent's eyes for some moments. Then he looked out the window and frowned. When he again looked at Brent it was with a certain measure of respect.

"I think I understand you," he said. "An' maybe I better go out there with you. You still want to work on that ranch?"

"Not with your assistance," answered Brent.

The sheriff raised his brows. "But you're askin' me to help you get your saddle," he pointed out.

"I'm protectin' myself an' Lawton," said Brent coldly.

Furness drummed on his desk with his fingers a few moments. "I'll step over an' see Jim Lynch a minute an' then we'll go out," he said, rising.

"I reckon I wouldn't do that," said Brent sharply.

"Why not?" asked the sheriff quickly.

Brent put his hands on his hips and looked squarely at the other. "Sheriff," he said slowly, "how long have you known there isn't any Long Pete?"

Ed Furness never batted an eye. "Since I saw the first note he was supposed to have left," he replied.

Brent smiled, and his eyes twinkled. "You ain't got any ideas about his—his ghost, have you?" he suggested.

"If I have, I'm keepin' 'em to myself," Furness returned.

"I reckon that reward is the straight goods, Ed."

"It is. My name's signed to it."

"I suppose you can raise a bunch of men here on short notice for—special duty?" asked Brent.

"I didn't lose much time gettin' started after you," said Furness.

Brent reached in a pocket and drew out an object. He laid it on the desk. The sheriff looked at it and saw a blue poker check with the white outlines of a miniature Goddess of Liberty on it. He looked at Brent questioningly.

"If a messenger brings you that reminder of the blue-cloth tables, Sheriff, you hustle your bunch an' beat it where he, she or it tells you." With which remark Brent replaced the check in his pocket.

Furness regarded him closely. "You seen the ghost?" he asked, almost politely.

"You can't put your fingers on a ghost, Ed—but you can pay rewards on one! Are you ready to start?"

"Yes, we'll go," decided Furness.

They went to the barn for their horses and in a few minutes were riding at a fast gallop for the Rabbit Foot Ranch. They rode half the distance before a word was spoken. It was Brent who broke the silence.

"The thing I can't understand, Sheriff, is what

you were doin' out at that spring east of here the day I arrived in the country."

"If you'd been a little sooner you'd have caught me tacking up that reward notice on the cottonwood tree," replied Furness.

Brent grinned amiably. "I see now why you wear a derby hat," he said.

For the first time during their association, Sheriff Ed Furness smiled in genuine pleasure. "You said that thinking I'd tell you, Brent; but I'm not goin' to do it."

When they arrived at the ranch, Furness asked at once for Lawton. They found the Rabbit Foot foreman in his little office in the front of the ranch house.

"This man wants his saddle and bridle," said Furness to Lawton in a businesslike voice.

Lawton looked keenly at Brent, but gave no sign that he was thinking of what had taken place the night before. Brent waited for him to tell the sheriff of the shooting of the man west of the butte, but Lawton made no mention of it.

"Sure," he said. "Come right along and I'll get it." He led the way out of the house to the barn.

Brent was puzzled. Hadn't he shot one of the Rabbit Foot men? And if he had, why should Lawton choose to conceal the fact? Perhaps the explosion would come later.

Lawton pointed to the saddle and bridle on a peg near the door. "Help yourself," he said.

Brent brought his horse and quickly changed saddles and bridles. "This outfit belongs to Carman," he said as he hung the other bridle and saddle on the peg. "I reckon you'll see that he gets 'em when he comes down again or maybe I'll take 'em back later." He saw Lawton's eyes narrow.

But the Rabbit Foot foreman recovered and smiled at Furness. "Nice day," he said. "Did this gent swear out a warrant?"

The sheriff shook his head. "He was figurin' on coming after his property alone, an' I thought I might as well ride out. Ain't taking on any new hands?"

"Not recent," said Lawton, without looking at Brent. "Had some applications, but I ain't looked up the references."

Brent swung into the saddle. "Where's Nagel, the cow boss?" he asked Lawton.

"On the lower range," replied Lawton, frowning.

"So long, Ed," said Brent cheerily.

"Where you goin'?" demanded the sheriff.

"I'm goin' down an' see Nagel an' report for work," Brent called over his shoulder as he tickled his horse with his spurs and galloped away.

CHAPTER ELEVEN
Slippery Range

Brent reported to Nagel, showed him the letter he had retrieved from the floor of the Carman cabin the night before, and then waited for orders.

Nagel looked at his horse with a grin. "Expect that's a good hoss for cuttin' out," he said.

"He can get in among 'em," said Brent. "All I've got to do is point out the cow an' calf I want out of the bunch an' then I can go to sleep."

"Did Lawton send you down?"

"Nope. He saw the letter first, though. He was talkin' with the sheriff an' I asked where you was an' came on down."

"Wasn't you the man that made the hoss deal with Lawton?" Nagel asked.

"I was," replied Brent.

"An' the sheriff chased you, caught you an' made you go to work, eh?" said Nagel with a coarse laugh.

Brent winked. "The sheriff ain't given me any orders that's bothered me," he said. "But I don't mind workin' cows."

Nagel laughed again. "All right. Slope down there where that lower bunch of whitefaces is an' see they don't get too close to the Mexican border."

"Which ain't more'n a thousand mile south, I reckon," answered Brent, grinning. "I've ridden it."

"You from down that way?" asked Nagel, interested.

"I've played it from Sierra Blanca to Nogales," boasted Brent. "An' I've seen longhorns blown clean across the Rio Grande by dust storms." He rode off, leaving Nagel sitting his horse looking after him.

"I had an idea," he muttered to himself. "This crowd has been in those same dust storms. He knew what I meant; I saw it in his eye. An' that sheriff is wiser than Billy-be-damn!" he concluded in a tone of admiration.

He worked the rest of the day without seeing Lawton. That night Nagel ordered him to the bunk house.

"Won't break you in night work yet," he said, looking sharply at Brent.

"I've been known to see things in the dark— an' miss others," was Brent's only comment.

For the next three days he was on the southernmost part of the range. He saw Lawton, but the foreman took no notice of him. Nor did he hear anything of any Rabbit Foot man having been shot. The men in the bunk house were close-mouthed and eyed him surreptitiously. He, in turn, seemed to take no notice of them, although he was studying them closely.

When a week had passed Lawton rode down to see him. "Sheriff told me your letter was all right," he said coldly.

"Glad you got your references," Brent retorted.

"You must have some kind of a pull with the old man," Lawton commented.

"Think so?" Brent inquired. "He asked me to go to work for him the first day I hit town."

"So I hear," said Lawton, leaning on his saddle horn. "I reckon Miss Carol thinks you're a top hand, too."

"She ain't had much chance to get acquainted with me," said Brent, looking him in the eye.

"Don't know but what she wants to know you better," said Lawton with the ghost of a smile.

"That's her privilege, any time," said Brent.

"Guess to-night's as good a time as any, then," suggested Lawton. "Report at my office at six o'clock." And he rode away leaving Brent scowling in perplexity.

"Now, what's the play?" he asked himself. "Lawton maybe thinks he has me thinkin' he's actin' natural, but I ain't been eatin' loco so's he could notice it."

When he walked into Lawton's office at the ranch house at six o'clock, the foreman scowled as though he had to give an order that was distasteful to him.

"Get your supper, slick up a bit—if you want to—an' beat it on into town," he said crisply. "I think there's a dance or something in there to-night."

"So? How many of the boys are goin' in?"

"Just you an' Nagel," said Lawton with a half sneer. "I expect you'll be guests of honor."

"Invitation from his nibs, the big boss?" inquired Brent jovially.

"Go do as you're told an' don't be standing there askin' questions," snarled out Lawton. "You're not receivin' invitations; you're takin' orders!"

"An' this ought to be an easy order to fill," Brent shot back over his shoulder as he departed.

He left the ranch with Nagel soon after supper. The cow boss seemed in a happy mood and explained that he only got one chance for a visit to town, except on business, between the spring round-up and the fall beef shipment.

"We'll make a night of it," he said with a wink. "You do the dancin' an' I'll look after the pasteboards. I reckon we're both gamblin', only—"

"I don't know what you're talkin' about," said Brent coldly.

Nagel laughed loudly. But Brent was trying to figure it all out. Had Carol Lynch told her uncle she would like to see him again and had her uncle ordered Lawton to send him in to a dance? It seemed preposterous. Yet in their only meeting, Brent had divined that Carol Lynch was a girl of spirit. An imp of devilment had lurked in her eyes. She might do such a thing as have him ordered into town if she felt a passing interest in him. He experienced a thrill, and then laughed at himsclf inwardly. Well, she was a mighty likable girl, and if she wanted him for a guest at a dance or a party—he was willing.

They galloped into town after dark and put up their horses at the barn. Nagel suggested that they visit one of the three resorts of Rangeview and Brent agreed. But with one drink, which he insisted on buying, Brent ended his activity in that quarter, and Nagel's arguments proved in vain.

Brent ascertained that there was indeed a dance in town that night, and that it had started. He had shed his chaps and spurs and gun at the barn and he now proceeded direct to the hall where the dance was being held, accompanied by Nagel, who said he "wanted to see what it looked like while he could still see."

The hall was a one-story building and was well filled when they arrived. Brent took up his position to one side of the door, and it was not long before he saw Carol Lynch. She saw him at the same time and left the bench, where she was the center of attraction between numbers, and came toward him.

"How do you do, Mr.—there, I came near saying it right out loud," she laughed in greeting, holding out her hand.

Brent took the hand, conscious that the red was burning through his tan.

"You might as well say it, ma'am; I reckon it wouldn't startle anybody."

"But it wouldn't be polite," she said; "for I'm giving this dance and you are one of the guests. Do you dance?"

"I dance at it," he answered her smilingly, "but it's been some while since I had any practice."

"Then you must start right now to get back into form." The orchestra had struck up, and she led him out on the floor. He still held his hat. He held it in the hand he put about her waist when they went into the dance.

"Did you send word out to the ranch for me to come in?" he asked as they began to waltz.

"There! He starts out dancing perfectly and asking questions. You are indeed accomplished, Mr. Brent."

"You mustn't jolly me, Miss Carol, because I'm a very serious-minded person. You see, I had a girl once who was a school-teacher—"

"I knew it," said the girl. "You're a top hand with the ladies as well as the men!"

"I see it's no use," he complained. "But I really would like to know if you sent an invitation out for me."

"All right—I did. Wasn't that all right?"

"It sure was, ma'am. I was wonderin' why."

"I wanted to tell you I'd heard some good things about you," she said.

"Somebody must have a good imagination, ma'am."

"Not unless it's the sheriff," she said merrily. "He told me how you insisted on protecting that young Carman boy."

"Shucks, that wasn't anything, ma'am. I got the boy in trouble an' it was up to me to try an' get him out of it again."

"Still, I'm inclined to believe you are more of a Samaritan than an outlaw, Mr. Brent."

"A Samaritan? That's a good word, Miss Carol. So first I'm an outlaw an' then I'm a Samaritan. *I* don't know which I like best!"

"Maybe you're both," she answered. "The 'Outlaw Samaritan.' I don't think you're all bad, Mr. Brent."

"Don't be too sure," he warned. "Did you invite Nagel, too?"

"Who is Nagel?"

"Our cow boss."

"Oh, I remember him. No, I guess I overlooked him. Is he here, too? I don't see how Mr. Lawton can spare two such valuable men at once. Last fall when he was in to a dance this Pete person made away with some cattle."

Brent sobered. The dance was over, and he led her to her seat. She was immediately surrounded and told him she would introduce him around.

"You'll have to excuse me, Miss Carol. I'm holding my hat." With that he backed away and retreated behind the ring of admirers that formed about her.

He did not see Nagel on the way out, but he met the sheriff.

"Ed, I'm a Samaritan!" he said to that astonished official. "But I'm still packin' the blue check!"

He hurried down the street and in the shadows near the barn he stopped to think. Nagel hadn't been invited. Had Lawton sent him along to keep an eye on him, Brent? And cattle had been stolen when Lawton was at a dance the fall before!

Brent hurried into the barn. He put on his chaps and spurs and gun. Jake, the barn man, was out and Brent bridled and saddled his horse. He led him out the rear door and through the trees to the prairie. Then he mounted, drove in his spurs, and raced like mad in the direction of Rabbit Butte.

CHAPTER TWELVE
Hunches Win

Brent rode as swift as the gallant horse could carry him. Straight for the butte at first, and then in a northwesterly direction toward the bad lands.

"Maybe we're wrong, old hoss," he cried aloud; "but we're goin' to play our hunches to win."

In less than two hours he was in the shadow of the tumbled ridges and gnarled trees north of the butte. He rode in around the fence on the trail by which he had first entered the bad lands. He followed this trail until he came to the intersection where the other trail led to the gate in the fence. He turned into this trail and proceeded slowly until he reached the gate. There he halted in the shadow of the trees and looked at the north side of the butte and listened. Faint noises came to his ears—dull echoes that barely sounded on the light breeze.

He watched for half an hour and then turned and retraced his way along the trail. But when he reached the intersection he did not turn. He kept on the trail to the north. He quickened his pace, for his horse was sure-footed; took advantage of every starlit meadow to urge his mount into a gallop. And finally he came to the meadow where was located the Carman cabin.

He galloped to the door, dismounted, and entered unceremoniously. The fact that the door was not barred was proof that Carman was not there, that the boy had left the door unbarred in anticipation of his father's return.

He struck a match and looked into the bedroom. The boy was asleep in one of the bunks. The other bunk was unoccupied. Brent woke the youth.

"Alan," he said as soon as he had lighted a lamp and the boy was thoroughly awake, "will you do something for me? Something to-night—now?"

The boy nodded, struck by the earnestness of Brent's manner.

"All right, get your clothes on in a hurry, son."

While the boy was dressing, Brent took out a handkerchief, dropped into it the blue poker check with the white impression of the miniature Goddess of Liberty, and tied the handkerchief in a knot.

He gave it to the boy when he was ready. "Put that away in a pocket, son, where you won't lose it." He watched while the boy obeyed. "Now get your hoss an' ride like the devil himself was after you till you get to town. Leave your hoss any-where an' find Ed Furness. Give that knotted handkerchief to Ed, tell him to look into it an' to come to the lower trail into the rough country north of Rabbit Butte. Do you understand, son?"

The boy nodded soberly and repeated his instructions.

"All right, Alan," said Brent, taking the boy's hand. "Now ride as fast as you can, an' find Ed Furness as fast as you can, an' tell him as fast as you can. He'll know what to do. Then you take your hoss to the barn, go to the hotel an' get yourself a room an' some sleep, or come back slow—just as you like."

He stuffed a bill into the boy's boot top. "While you're gone, I'm goin' to try to do something good for your dad an' you. Now slope, son!"

The boy went out on the run and disappeared in the shadows on his way to the hidden horse corral.

Brent mounted and rode back the south trail, past the first intersection, to the intersection where the trail led up to the crest of the high ridge. He climbed this, and on the top he dismounted and looked below to the south.

Cattle were on the move!

Other shadows sped swiftly on either side of the strung-out herd—riders keeping the cattle in hand.

Brent kept his gaze on these riders, straining his eyes to watch them. Finally one, riding more slowly than the rest, came down from the north-west corner, halfway between the herd and the fence.

Brent flung himself on his horse and rode down the ridge. He dashed along the trail to the gate and sent his horse flying over it. Then he raced toward this lone rider and was upon him in the shadows almost before the other was aware of his nearness.

"Carman!" he said in a sharp undertone, bringing his horse around in front of the man's mount.

He rode in close to the man on the right and took his gun from its holster and slipped it into a pocket.

"Now we'll go on to your place."

They rode at a brisk jog along the trail north until they reached the meadow and the cabin. At the door they dismounted and left the horses with reins dangling. Carman lighted a lamp.

Brent looked at him sternly. "Now tell me about it as quickly as you can," he commanded. "The game's up, Carman; my hunches have all proved to be the goods. I got you out of that because there's goin' to be the devil to pay sooner'n anybody expects, an' I got you out because of your boy."

Carman stared at him dully for nearly half a minute. He looked toward the darkened bedroom and Brent shook his head.

"I've sent him away," he said quietly.

Carman buried his face in his hands. Then he looked up almost with defiance. "I wanted to get a start," he said in a thick voice. "It was for him as much as anything else. But I took the wrong trail. I saw a chance that looked good, an' I took thirty Rabbit Foot steers. I left the first Long Pete note. Lawton caught me an' then he had me. But I was wise to his game, too, an'—but I had to help him.

It drove me to drink, but he let me keep the steers an'—"

The man broke down and Brent looked away, his eyes flashing.

"Listen," said Brent, "put that light out an' stay here, understand?"

Carman nodded in a paroxysm of grief.

Brent laid the man's gun on the table, blew out the light in the lamp, and hurried out. He threw himself into the saddle and galloped across the meadow into the trail. This time he took the trail to the left when he reached the first intersection, and after a time he came out at the southeast end of the bad lands, around the fence.

To eastward he saw a number of bobbing shadows, and he raced to meet them. The shadows took form, appeared as horses, and Brent swept up with his hat held aloft as a signal.

"Long Pete's movin' his cattle north," he said to Sheriff Ed Furness, who was in the lead of a posse of a dozen men. "Trailin' 'em from the north side of the butte to the northwest corner of the open range an' into the foothills. Quite a string."

Ed Furness looked at him with a squint for a moment. Then he turned in the saddle and gave a number of hurried orders. The posse swept on. When they reached the southeast corner of the bad lands they split into two groups. One group rode west along the fence and the other dashed for the north side of the butte. Brent rode with Furness along the fence.

Before the riders with the cattle, preoccupied with their work to a certain extent, realized what was happening, the riders along the fence had passed them. Furness, Brent, and the others closed in. The line of moving cattle broke, and the herd began to bunch. Then shots sounded from north of the butte.

Everywhere on the triangle of range north of the butte the shadows were pierced by red streaks of fire. The cattle snorted, bellowed, and began to run. Some of the riders were caught in front of the stampeding herd and were forced to flee toward the members of the posse nearest the butte. The rest of the posse dashed for the riders who were left behind in the open. Guns barked and horses raced. In the northwest corner sounded other shots, and Brent saw a lone rider dashing toward him. He recognized him by his bulk in the saddle and his great horse. It was Lawton.

He spurred the dun toward the oncoming rider, raised in the stirrups, and brought up his gun. Lawton fired—once, twice, three times at long range. Then he dashed eastward with Brent in pursuit. Ed Furness came down from the west. But the black was too much for either of the pursuers' horses. He left them behind, lost them, and disappeared in the shadows of the bad lands.

The first gray glimmer of dawn was in the east as Brent and Furness met.

"We've got 'em pretty well rounded up," said Furness, "except Lawton. We'll have to comb the bad lands for him an' keep watch in the north, I guess. How'd you find out they had the cattle cached on top of the butte? I didn't know till tonight there was a way up there."

"I lost a herd up here a few days ago," said Brent absently. "Then I caught sight of a fire on top the butte from that high ridge where he spent the night after I met him in Carman's cabin, an'—" He bit off his words and cried out:

"I forgot! He'll probably pass Carman's cabin —it's on the best trail north. But he won't pass it—he'll look in." He stared at Ed Furness.

"Well, what of it?" asked Furness.

"What of it? Why, Carman's there!"

Brent spurred his horse toward the gate in the early dawn with Furness in hot pursuit. He jumped the gate and galloped into the trail, keeping the dun at a breakneck pace. He reached the meadow and raced for the cabin door where Lawton's big black was standing with reins dangling. As he flung himself from the saddle the roar of a gun came from within. Brent leaped to the door.

Frank Carman was lying, face downward, on the floor. Lawton was standing with one hand on the table, his gun hand, grasping the weapon that still smoked, hanging at his side. His eyes, when he met those of Brent, were pin points of red fire. His lips curled in a sneer. He saw that Brent's gun was in its holster.

"That's what he gets for double crossin' his pardner an' spillin' the works to you, you rat!" he said hoarsely.

"You're wrong, Lawton," said Brent. "I had a hunch about you from the start. Then I saw a bunch of cattle vanish at the north end of the butte. Next, two men chased me down there an' I plugged one of 'em an' you never peeped. The night I left you here I went to the top of the ridge west of the gate. I saw a fire on top of the butte an' *I saw you go up there!*"

"Smart," sneered Lawton. "An' you came on an' took the job to keep an eye on us, eh?" His face was livid.

"You guessed it, Lawton. What's more, you knew it all the time. But *I* knew I'd have to catch you in the act of movin' those cattle, for they were still on Rabbit Foot range when they was on top of the butte. You were slick. A little remark a lady passed at the dance last night gave me a tip that you'd sent Nagel in to watch me an' see I stayed there while you got the cattle out. I had a hunch Nagel would play the bars too strong, an' even that hunch came true."

Lawton leaned toward him, his eyes blazing, his lips purple.

"Have you got a hunch now?"

"Yes, but it's up to you to make it come true. Drop that gun, Lawton!"

Brent leaped into the air as Lawton's gun struck up. Then the cabin seemed to burst with sound as two weapons roared almost together. Lawton sank down, his head striking against the table. He toppled on the floor. Brent leaned against the door jamb and smiled wanly at Sheriff Ed Furness, who looked in with an expression of utter amazement on his face.

CHAPTER THIRTEEN
A Collection

It was morning in the tumbled lands north of Rabbit Butte. The scrub pines, buck brush, stunted cedars, willows and scattered cottonwoods were a vivid green in the brilliant rays of the sun. Grouse strutted in the fragrant meadows; wild canaries and meadow larks flew like flaming darts of color; a scented breeze filtered down through the hills.

Steve Brent stood in the doorway of the Carman cabin looking out upon the world with a troubled look in his eyes. In the meadow his rangy dun horse cropped the luscious grass. Behind him, in the large room of the cabin, there were sounds suggestive of the washing of dishes.

Brent turned and looked at the boy who was attending to the domestic tasks that are the aftermath of breakfast. It was four days since Frank Carman had been shot to death by Bill Lawton, renegade foreman of the Rabbit Foot. Carman had been buried the day after, and the boy had displayed a fortitude that had won Brent's heart. Since then, Brent had tried to keep the lad's mind occupied with other things than thought of his father's mistake and death.

They had rounded up and returned the thirty head of cattle Carman had taken from the Rabbit

Foot. They had sold all of Carman's horses, except the one the boy rode, to the ranch. They had packed up the father's effects for storage in town. They had walked and ridden together and had had long talks.

"Alan, what do you reckon you want to do?" asked Brent, after clearing his throat.

"I want to go away from here," replied the boy without hesitation. "I've been hemmed in by these brakes a long time, it seems like. I want to get out where I can see some country."

He looked up at Brent with a wistful expression. Brent threw away the butt of a cigarette and hastily rolled a new one.

"Do you know where you want to go?" he inquired as he lighted his smoke.

"Sure I do. I want to go with you, Steve." The boy's eyes were glowing as he looked into Brent's.

Brent stopped in his tracks. "Why, sonny, you don't know where I'm goin'—I don't know myself!"

Alan laughed joyously. "I don't care," he declared. "You won't get lost, will you?"

Brent grinned, but sobered right afterward. "Might be all right for us to travel together for the rest of the summer," he said. "But you ought to have some schoolin', Alan. Now don't shake your head, young fellow; I didn't have much schoolin' myself, an' that's why I know it's a good thing." He eyed the boy with mock severity, although he meant what he said.

Alan took one of his hands. "You wasn't figurin' on runnin' off an' leaving me, was you, Steve? I seen you lookin' at that dun horse."

Brent looked about the sunlit meadow. "How old are you, Alan?"

"Going on fourteen; but I'm big, ain't I—for how old I am?"

"You're quite a youngster," Brent affirmed. "You'll probably grow up into a man an' break some woman's heart with your good looks." He turned in the direction of the cabin.

"I've got to run in to town this mornin'," he said. "You hang aroun' till I get back."

"I'll get your horse ready," said the boy, starting on the run.

Two hours later Steve Brent sauntered into the office of Ed Furness, sheriff of Rabbit Butte County. The official was at his desk.

"Mornin', Ed," he greeted. "Nice day. I could hardly push my way into town, the meadow larks was so thick."

The sheriff tipped back his derby and looked at his visitor appraisingly. "Thought you'd probably left the country," he said, caressing his mustache.

"It ain't good policy to start anywhere else till you've finished your business where you're at, Ed," said Brent amiably. "Our business started when you tacked that notice on the cottonwood tree out by the big spring east of here."

The sheriff smiled to himself, drew a paper

from a drawer of his desk, and passed it to Brent.

"There's a voucher for a thousand—the county's half of the reward," he said. "Lynch is county treasurer."

"Thanks," said Brent, folding the paper and putting it in a pocket. "I suppose Jim's in town?"

"He's over in his bank," said Furness. "He may make you wait till the end of the month for that, though. It might cut into the interest or something."

"Well, now, maybe I can think of a way to circumvent him," drawled Brent. "There's a good word, Ed; that was number twenty. I lost my school-marm right after I learned that one."

"Who'd she marry?" asked Furness with a grin.

"The town banker," said Brent dryly. "Well, so long, Ed."

"Wait a minute," said the sheriff, rising from his chair. "What you goin' to do now, Brent?"

Brent slowly rolled a cigarette. "Ed, did you ever notice the cottonwoods when they're sheddin'? Know those little white veils they send driftin' on the wind? I see you do. You ought to; you live here. Well, Ed, sometimes those flecks of cotton will come settlin' down to the ground pretty as pretty. An' sometimes one'll go rearin' up in the air and float away. Seems as though you just can't tell what one of them cotton specks is goin' to do. Kind of interesting to watch 'em, Ed. Some folks is just like that."

"Why don't you stay here?" said Ed, frowning. "By George, I'll make you a deputy!"

"I'm packin' all I can carry, Ed," returned Brent. "A star on my shirt would plumb weigh me down!"

"Well, think it over," said Furness, offering his hand. "I won't ask for any—references."

"You've had 'em a long time," said Brent cheerfully, as he took the sheriff's hand.

He walked down the street to the bank. Then he entered the door and strode to Lynch's private office in the rear. He found the banker at his desk and tossed the voucher for one thousand dollars on the blotter before him.

"In fifties, if you've got 'em," he said briskly.

"These vouchers are payable at the end of the month," said the banker, examining the slip of paper.

"I didn't wait till the end of the month to find out who was stealin' your cattle," Brent pointed out. "If I had, the whole bunch would be across the line by now."

"Ahem!" Lynch looked at him quizzically. "You want to open an account with this?"

"I've got room for it in my clothes," Brent drawled out. "I got more room than time."

"You're leaving?" asked Lynch in surprise.

"Mebbe. Let's settle our business before your clerk gets so nervous with me in here that he can't count."

Lynch rose, went out into the banking room, and soon returned with a packet of bills which he handed to Brent.

"You can count it," he said.

"I'll take your word for it," said Brent cheerfully. "An' now I'll take the other thousand."

Lynch raised his brows. "There's no other thousand," he said quietly.

Brent's eyes hardened. "I thought we'd be able to avoid an argument," he said slowly. "That notice said two thousand for Long Pete, Jim, an' you told me yourself it was one thousand from the county an' one from you."

"But you didn't get Long Pete," said Lynch. You couldn't get him because there wasn't no such person. An' if I hadn't offered you a job out there, an' give it to you later, you wouldn't have got the thousand from the county."

"Listen, Jim." Brent's voice was chilly, but clear. His eyes had narrowed. "If there's anything I won't argue about, Jim, it's money. You fork over the thousand or I'll just naturally take it away from you!"

His right hand moved in the wink of an eye and his gun covered the banker.

"I was goin' to offer you a good job on the ranch," said Lynch darkly.

"Well, you sure went about it a poor way," said Brent grimly. "Trot out that other thousand, Lynch, an' don't waste no time doin' it."

The banker moved toward the banking room.

"I've—I've got it ready," stammered the clerk, thrusting a packet of bills toward Lynch.

"Right over his shoulder," called Brent. "That's the boy. Now there's a well-trained clerk, Jim," he chuckled as he put the bills in his pocket. "He don't believe in arguments no more'n *I* do."

"The argument would have terminated in your favor whether you'd drawn your gun or not," snapped out the banker, turning back to his desk. "An', anyway, I'm much obliged."

"Thanks, Jim. Next time you see Ed Furness tell him that last word I slipped him is a good one to remember."

Steve Brent rode into the meadow in the bad lands whistling merrily. He saw a horse in one of the corrals back of the cabin. Then Alan Carman came to the door to greet him.

"Pack what you want to take with you, sonny, an' we'll be on our way," he sang out.

"It's all rolled in my slicker an' on the back of my saddle," said the boy with a glad smile. "I'm ready to go, Steve."

Brent's eyes sparkled. "All right, saddle up!"

Three quarters of an hour later they rode out of the tumbled country to the flowing plain and turned north toward the purple cones of the Sweetgrass hills, a hundred miles away.

CHAPTER FOURTEEN
Man and Boy

They were making a noon-day camp under the banks of a coulee where there was a natural spring, a sward of rich, green grass, and a healthy stand of willows with stately cottonwoods towering above. The warm sun filtered through the branches and scattered golden spangles on the verdant carpet where the man knelt by a small fire and busied himself with coffeepot and frying pan. The boy sat on the grass with his hands clasped about his doubled knees. The horses grazed in the shade with bridle reins dangling and saddle cinches loosened.

"Why don't you let me help, Steve?" the boy complained, rocking to and fro. "I can cook."

"I know it, Alan," was the reply. "When we're inside, you do the cookin'; when we're outside, I'll do it. That's a fifty-fifty proposition, an' that's the way we're travelin'."

The boy's eyes glowed. It was plain that he entertained a feeling of respect and admiration for the tall, gray-eyed, clean-skinned man with the bronze-colored hair and the flashing smile. Indeed, it would not have been a figment of the imagination for one watching them to assume that the boy loved his companion.

"We're pardners, ain't we, Steve?" said the youth in a happy tone.

"I reckon we are, Alan." Steve looked at him curiously. "An' you're the first pardner I ever had."

The boy made a pretense of looking after their horses to be doing something; then came at the other's call and sat down by the cool spring to eat.

"I brought Pa's gun along," said Alan with a quick glance at his friend. "It's in my slicker pack."

"So?" Steve Brent looked at the boy's face closely, but the lad did not raise his eyes.

"I thought maybe you'd teach me to draw an' shoot," the boy went on. "I'm nearly fourteen. Ain't it time I started to learn?"

Brent frowned. It did no good to recollect that Frank Carman had been shot and killed by a cow-thief foreman because he was not quick enough with that same gun his son had mentioned. Under the circumstances, it would be hard to lecture the boy on the evils of gun play. And Steve Brent felt a sudden yearning to teach the boy the trick of his own lightning draw. Taken at that age—fourteen—and carefully tutored, Alan Carman could become one of the most formidable gun experts in the north range country in a very few years.

"What do you want to learn to draw an' shoot for, Alan?" asked Brent.

"Why—it's a good thing to know, ain't it?" said the boy, surprised.

Brent shrugged. "Yes—an' no. It's accordin' to how you use your knowledge, sonny. It don't hurt a man none in this country to be fast on the draw, I reckon; sometimes it's a sort of protection. But it's dangerous to be too fast, unless you've got a good level head. Do you reckon you've got a level head, son?"

The boy looked up soberly. "What do you think, Steve?"

Brent's gaze met the frank, brown eyes. He noted the youth's clean-cut features, the high forehead under the shock of chestnut hair. Alan would grow up into a mighty handsome man. It was also dangerous for a man to be handsome in that country—as in any other. But it was the light in the boy's eyes that convinced him.

"I reckon you're capable of ridin' on an even keel, son," he said, "but you'll have to promise me something before I'll consider teachin' you to draw."

"What is it, Steve?" asked the boy quietly. "What do you want me to promise?"

"I want you to promise me that you'll never start any trouble on your own accord, son. I want you to promise that you'll never throw your gun on a man unless it's to protect a woman, an' that—if you *do* get into trouble—you'll never draw first."

The boy thought for a minute as if he was adjusting his mind to all angles of the pact Brent suggested.

"Suppose I'd get to be a sheriff or something," he said earnestly.

Brent smothered a laugh and frowned. "I hope you never will," he said. "But I'm exceptin' the law—when you're on its side."

"I'll promise, Steve," Alan finally answered.

"Shake on it an' remember when pardners shake on anything it's a right sacred thing," said Brent.

The boy took his hand in his warm clasp and Brent saw that the ceremony meant much to him. Brent knew the lad would keep his word.

"Now you can wash the things up," Brent suggested when they were through. "That's another part of our fifty-fifty play, son."

When he had finished, the boy dropped down on the grass in the shade beside Brent.

"Now, let's see," said Brent, exhaling cigarette smoke in a thin cloud. "We've been ridin' north three days since we left your dad's place down in the bad lands near Rabbit Butte. 'Member I told you when your dad died an' you wanted to come along that I wasn't sure where I was goin'? Well, I ain't sure yet. But we ought to be coming to the high line of the railroad an' a town up here pretty quick."

"There's a town up here called Shelton," the boy volunteered. "They used to drive cattle from the Rabbit Foot Ranch up here to ship."

"Shelton's the town," Brent said. "We'll take a look aroun' there, an' if the range don't suit us, we'll move on. It's hard for me to stay put, I reckon; but we'll have to see that you get settled somewheres by fall, for you've got to have some schoolin', son."

"Couldn't you teach me, Steve?"

Brent laughed harshly. Then the red burned through his tan. "Didn't you bring the belt an' holster?"

The boy flushed and ran back for belt and holster which he quickly put on. Then he shoved the gun in its sheath and was ready for his first lesson.

Brent picked up a round rock about four inches in diameter and put it in the crotch of a cotton-wood branch where it joined the trunk of the tree.

"Can you crack that?" he asked the boy.

Alan drew out the heavy weapon, and fired. The rock was shattered.

"Well, now, that ain't so bad," approved his instructor. "We'll try one a bit smaller."

The boy hit the second rock and the third. Then Brent put up a rock of the same size as the first target.

"Try that," he said, "with your hand down a ways—say halfway between your shoulder an' your belt."

The boy followed his instructions as to the holding of the gun, and fired. He missed. Twice again he fired and missed the target, and he flushed with chagrin.

"Now, son," drawled out Brent, "you're lookin' half at the target an' half at the end of your gun. Look at what you're shootin' at an' don't pay any attention to the gun a-tall."

Alan tried again and missed. But with the third shot he split the rock.

"That might have been an accident," said Brent. "But you're catchin' on. It'll take time, son. We've got to get that gun down to your hip with you hittin' the mark every time. Then we'll start on the draw. It takes patience an' a lot of cartridges. If you've got the patience, I'll supply the shells. I reckon we've done enough for to-day."

He had hardly finished speaking when three horsemen dashed up the coulee and reined in their horses near himself and the boy. Alan still held the gun in his hand.

The first of the riders, evidently the leader, twisted in his saddle and eyed the boy with an amused grin.

"What you doin', kid, trainin' your eye or your hand?"

"Both," was the boy's retort as he looked at the man coldly.

"All right, hit that hat," said the man as he spun his hat in the air.

Alan's gun came up and he fired. The hat seemed to jump in the air and the boy's eyes flashed with pride. It was the quickest and best shot he'd ever made.

The man in the saddle swore roundly while his two companions winked at each other, but didn't laugh.

"You've put a hole in that hat!" yelled the man with a curse directed at the boy.

Brent sauntered to the boy's side and stood a little in front of him.

"What'd you want him to do?" he asked pleasantly.

"I didn't think the brat could hit it!" the man explained.

"I didn't either," said Brent. "But he did, an' that's what you asked him to do. You've been accommodated, so why all the cussin'?"

The man dismounted and picked up his hat. There was a hole through the high crown. He scowled darkly at the boy, jammed the hat on his head, and turned on Brent. His big, swarthy face was dark with anger, although there was curiosity in the small, beady eyes that were like black buttons under his heavy brows. He put his hands on his hips. He was a big man, and he wore a gun and an air of supreme arrogance.

"Who're you?" he demanded.

"Steve Brent's my name," replied Brent coolly.

"Where from?"

"South—anywhere south, so long's it's far enough."

"Where you goin'?"

"North—to the first town."

"Fair enough. I take it you don't know many people aroun' here."

"Nope. An' I ain't makin' any new acquaintances just at present." Brent looked the man in the eye and the man turned to regard his companions with a grin.

"Hear that, Snally?"

One of the two riders, a thin man with a pale face and blue eyes that shifted nervously as he toyed with his reins, smiled, disclosing a row of yellow teeth.

"Ain't what I'd call neighborly," he said, with a faint sneer on his thin white lips.

"What do you think, Royce?" asked the leader, speaking to the other rider.

Royce pulled at his drooping black mustaches and looked at Brent out of cold, glittering black eyes.

"Cowhand," he grunted. "Playin' safe."

"Did you hear that?" the leader asked Brent with a scowl.

"Eh?" said Brent, as though he had been startled out of a reverie. "Oh, yes, I heard him. I ain't deaf, but I was wonderin' about something."

"Wonderin' about me?" asked the other.

"Nope. I was wonderin' if this here spring stays wet all summer."

The man's eyes flashed. "What if it does—you figure on usin' it?"

"Nope. Just thought maybe you'd know, which would show you knew the country an' how far it is to the nearest town." Brent raised his brows and looked at him. Something in his eyes held the other's. Then the man turned abruptly to his horse and mounted.

"Shelton's about fifteen miles north," he said, shaking out his reins. "Figure on goin' up there?"

"Sure thing," replied Brent. "Nice town?"

" 'Tis for them as treats it nice," replied the man. "You don't look like you'd stir it up none."

"Oh, I'm plumb peaceable," said Brent with an idle gesture.

"You didn't ask me who I was," said the man, frowning.

"You want to be asked?" inquired Brent.

"You'll find out quick enough—an' keep that kid in his cradle!" With a laugh of derision the man whirled his horse and the trio galloped up the coulee toward the spring.

Brent said nothing as he and Alan walked to their horses and tightened the saddle cinches. The boy replaced his belt and gun in his slicker pack and they mounted. They rode out of the coulee behind the three horsemen. Soon they were jogging north on the plain.

"Ask him who he was!" exclaimed Brent to himself. "I've heard too many descriptions of 'Snag' Dorgan not to recognize him on sight. But what's that gun-fightin', card-cheatin', outlaw free-booter doin' up this way?"

He pulled the brim of his hat down to shade his eyes from the burning sun and rode on with a puzzled face.

CHAPTER FIFTEEN
Treated Nice

For an hour they rode silently. Brent was busy with his thoughts, and the boy was strangely exhilarated, both with an apparent interest in the country—showing that it was the farthest he had been away from home—and because of his unexpected showing at pistol practice in shooting a hole through the stranger's hat.

In another hour they saw a thin spiral of smoke on the prairie ahead.

"I reckon that's Shelton," called Brent, pointing. "We'll go on in."

They spurred their horses, and soon the town was discernible, with its setting of cottonwoods and willows along a thin stream. The smoke spiral had flattened on the horizon to northward, showing that a train had just left.

When they rode into the short, dusty main street of the town, they kept on past the wooden structures that lined it on either side until they came to a hotel with a livery barn next to it at the farther end. They rode to the barn and put up their horses. Then they repaired to the hotel with their slicker packs and Brent engaged a large, double room on the second floor in front. They put the packs in the room, washed, and went downstairs.

They had just gained the small lobby opening onto the street when the front door opened and one of the men they had met at the spring south of town, entered. They recognized the man the leader had addressed as Snally. The man scarcely looked at them, and then went to the desk where he busied himself at the register, paid some money, and went out.

"Reckon we're goin' to have our friends with us in this hotel," Brent said with a frown. "Well, we can keep away from them." He looked at Alan with a puzzled expression.

"This is the first time we've been in town together, pardner," he said, "an' it's just come home to me that I don't know just what to do with you in town when I want to slip aroun' an' take in the sights."

"I'll go get something to eat," said the boy.

"All right, an' then you come back here in the lobby or go up to the room till I get a chance to look over the lay of the land. We may want to stay here a while an' we may want to move on. I reckon you don't care."

The boy laughed. "You're runnin' the excursion, Steve," he said with some excitement. "I'll go back to the room when I've fed up."

They went out, and Steve walked a few doors up the street with Alan to where there was a restaurant. He left the boy there and continued on up the street until he reached a large resort, evidently the most pretentious place of the kind in the town. He hesitated for a moment and then went in.

It was a typical rendezvous for men; a long room with a bar on one side, gambling tables on the other and in the rear. It was thronged with a picturesque crew of cow-punchers and sheepmen from near the line, railroad men, professional gamblers, and the riffraff of boosters and hangers-on that frequent places where money is freely spent.

One of the first men Brent saw at the bar was Snag Dorgan. This was because Dorgan was a large man, domineering and loud talking, a man who required plenty of room and who got it, and who naturally would be the central figure in any group such as would be gathered in a place of that kind. With Dorgan was another member of the trio Brent had met south of town, the man Dorgan had called Royce. They were drinking the white liquor that was being served.

Brent knew Dorgan didn't know him, except for their meeting of that day. He knew Dorgan didn't know that he, Brent, knew him. In this situation Brent had the advantage. He had heard much of the man in the south, and nothing to his good. He shrugged and turned his attention to the gaming tables where stud poker was being played, save for two tables in the rear where games of black-jack or twenty-one were in progress.

Soon he saw the man Snally. He smiled to himself.

"Playin' right up to form," he thought. "Snally is the card man of the outfit, Royce does the dirty work, an' Dorgan is the gun thrower when it comes to the show-down."

He watched Snally and soon saw that the white-faced man was a sharp of no mean ability. He manipulated the cards in his thin, tapering fingers with a smoothness and rapidity that protected his crooked deals with every other player at the table watching him very closely.

Brent watched his work with ill-bestowed admiration. The man was perfect! He was winning, too, as was natural under the circumstances. It was fascinating to note the precision with which he nipped certain amounts in checks off his stacks. He never counted them after he pushed them in the center; didn't look at them. He was like a machine, and his face was as inscrutable as human features could possibly be.

There was a vacant seat at the table, and Brent could not resist the impulse to sit in the game the better to watch this expert with the infallible fingers and the uncanny judgment.

When he sat down, Snally glanced at him casually. There was just a flicker of recognition, and he again turned to his cards. It was a matter of an instant, and was further proof of the man's superb control.

Brent played cautiously, winning a small pot, refusing to stay in the others until it came Snally's deal. He dealt Brent an ace for his hole card, and Brent stayed. On the second turn Brent received another ace, and Snally turned himself a queen for his first open card. Brent made a sizeable bet and one other player stayed with Snally.

The other man in the pot dropped out on the next round of cards when Brent received a jack and Snally a ten-spot. Again Brent bet, and Snally stayed. On the next turn Brent received a five and Snally turned up a nine for himself. He called Brent's bet. On the final turn Brent received a jack, making him two aces and two jacks, and Snally dealt himself a queen, making his hand show two queens in sight.

Brent made a light bet and Snally raised it twenty dollars. Brent took out tobacco and papers and rolled a cigarette. He lighted it with great deliberation.

"That's good," he said calmly.

Snally looked at him quickly, and his jaw dropped the fraction of an inch.

"Look what he passed up!" cried a booming voice behind Brent. Then a hand reached over his shoulder and turned his hole card, exposing the ace which made him two pair.

Quick as a wink Brent's hand struck across the table and he flipped up Snally's hole card. It was a queen, which made three queens in Snally's hand.

Snally snarled as Brent laughed softly. Then Brent kicked back his chair and rose. He found Snag Dorgan standing behind him, as he had expected. He merely glanced at the big man, picked up his checks, and walked to the bar to cash them.

Dorgan followed him with a sneer on his thick lips. He shoved in beside Brent as the latter received his money for his checks.

"When you goin' to buy that new hat to take the place of the one your kid punctured when he was playin' with that gun down there to-day?" he asked in a surly tone.

"When the wind quits blowin' through the holes," replied Brent coolly. He saw the man, Royce, edge in on the other side of him.

"Then I take it that holes in hats is the style up here," said Dorgan.

"If it is, you're settin' the style," returned Brent.

"Well, the rest of the bunch'll have to follow my lead," snarled out Dorgan, with a look and a nod at Royce.

Brent saw Royce reach for his, Brent's hat— caught a flash in the mirror of the man's hand starting for his head. Royce intended to throw Brent's hat in the air so Dorgan could shoot a hole in it. But Royce's hand did not reach its mark. Brent's left elbow shot back, catching Royce just under the chin and knocking him away from the bar. Brent turned around in a flash. There was a burst of astonished laughter from Dorgan.

Royce gathered himself in an instant. For a few moments he crouched, his lips working with rage, his black eyes glittering dangerously. Then he leaped at Brent, bringing a straight right with him.

Brent side-stepped and ducked and got in a left uppercut. Before the surprised Royce could recover, Brent sent home a right to the jaw that made Royce go staggering back to fall on the players at one of the tables. He slid and sprawled on the floor. Brent leaped toward him and kicked the gun that came into the man's hand. The gun struck the floor several feet away.

Stepping back, Brent saw Dorgan standing with his thumbs in the armholes of his vest, evidently enjoying the discomfiture of his companion on the floor.

He walked back to Dorgan's side. "Any more on the program this afternoon?" he inquired.

"Sure," said Dorgan heartily, much to Brent's surprise. "We'll have a little snort of this white-mule combination."

"No, thanks," said Brent curtly, and started for the door.

On the way out he saw that Snally had left the table where they had been playing. Outside the place Brent mentally upbraided himself for the affair. He had had no business to sit in the game, even though he had been fascinated by Snally's accomplishments. He didn't want trouble with Dorgan or Royce or Snally, although he thought of the latter with contempt. But why had Dorgan acted so pleased after the defeat of his friend?

Brent walked leisurely down to the hotel. He went in and started up the stairs. Before he reached the second floor he heard voices. Alan, the boy, was speaking.

"You can't come in," he was saying angrily. "I don't want to talk to you."

Brent went up the remaining stairs quickly. "Fast work, Snally," he said as he walked toward the open door of the room where the boy was standing, barring the way to the gambler.

Snally turned as if on a pivot. His white face seemed ghastly as he looked at Brent.

"Go right in," said Brent with a wave of the hand and a nod to the boy. "Go right in, Snally. Was you lookin' for me?"

The gambler wet his lips, hesitated, seemed about to take a long chance on flight, and then stepped into the room. Brent followed and closed the door. His look was no longer amiable when he stepped before Snally.

"Why did you come up here?" he asked crisply.

"To try an' find out who you was," Snally confessed. "You knew I had that third queen; you was wise to my work. It takes a good hand to get the low-down on me. You're clever yourself." It was apparent that he sought to pacify Brent by flattery, although he was too knowing to attempt to lie as to the reason for his visit to the room.

Brent knew that he spoke the truth. "I reckon you think I'm a shark like yourself," he said with a frown.

"I—wouldn't put it that way," said Snally with a smirk.

"Who's that big man with you fellows, the one that's bossin' the bunch, I mean?" Brent demanded.

"Him? Why that's Ed Brown, the sheepman." Snally rubbed his hands nervously.

Brent laughed. "Seems like Snag Dorgan is bound to take that little business down at the spring to heart," he said.

He saw Snally start at mention of the name. The gambler looked at him intently.

"Why didn't you tell him you knew him?" he asked in a thin voice.

"Because he might think it was strange," snapped out Brent. "Go down an' tell him that if he really feels he's entitled to a new hat, I'll buy it for him."

Snally sidled toward the door. His right hand caressed his left cuff, and Brent's lips curled in contempt. He knew the gambler had a small automatic or derringer up that cuff. He stepped past the man and opened the door for him.

"There's something else you can tell Dorgan,"

he said in an undertone. "I ain't makin' no announcements."

A smile that came close to being one of gratitude hung on the man's lips. Brent turned away in disgust as the gambler backed out the door, closing it behind him.

CHAPTER SIXTEEN
An Interview

Steve Brent sat down before the open window. The sun was sinking like a dazzling disk of gold behind the western peaks. A faint breeze stirred the dust of the street, rustled in the leaves of the cottonwoods, ruffled the white, muslin curtains of the window.

The boy took a chair opposite Brent and looked at him, his eyes wide and sober. Finally he spoke slowly.

"Steve, ain't I a bother to you?" he asked.

Brent looked at the boy, startled. Since he had practically adopted the youngster a few days before, after his father's untimely death, he had been obsessed with an unusual sense of responsibility. But it had never occurred to him that the lad was a bother.

Accustomed to traveling alone over great distances of open range and visiting isolated towns where he knew no one, the presence of a companion had furnished a new sensation—a sensation he had not been able to fathom. And he liked this upstanding youngster who had shot the hole in Snag Dorgan's hat without hesitation, and had been proud of it.

"Don't you be gettin' any such idea in your

head, Alan," he said firmly. "I'm just tryin' to figure out our next move. I reckon towns ain't right good places for us to hang aroun' in.

"We'll ride out a ways to-morrow, maybe down to that spring. That's a good isolated place, even if we did happen to run into that crowd to-day. An' say, son; if you see any of those fellows, don't speak to 'em or go near 'em."

The boy nodded, and they left the room, locked the door, and went down to the dining room.

After supper Brent found himself loath to leave the boy. They walked the length of the street in the twilight, and when darkness descended returned to the hotel. Brent read the small paper issued weekly in the town, while the boy, frankly tired, undressed and crept into the big bed.

Brent sat for some time after the boy had fallen asleep. The paper dropped from his knees to the floor unnoticed. The man looked curiously, time and again, at the features of the sleeping lad. A struggle appeared to be going on in his mind. At last he rose, blew out the light in the lamp, and let himself quietly out the door, locking it after him.

He strolled down the street on the opposite side. When he was across from the hotel, he stopped on the edge of the narrow sidewalk and looked up at the darkened windows of the room where the boy was sleeping. His eyes clouded and his brow wrinkled for a few moments as if he again considered a problem. Then he shrugged and smiled. The alert look came into his eyes once more when he gazed at the lighted windows of another room on the second floor of the hotel.

A man was sitting close to the window with his back toward it. He was leaning forward somewhat as if his arms were resting on a table. Once he turned so that his profile was outlined against the glow of the lamp. Brent recognized Snag Dorgan at once, and he surmised that the gambler, Snally, and probably Royce, were with him. This did not particularly interest him, but he noted carefully the location of the room and saw that it was at the west end of the building, several doors from his own.

He started to resume his walk, but found he could not continue it with ease while the three men were in the hotel so near to the lad, Alan. He went back to where he could keep an eye on the lighted room and see the darkened windows of his own. This feeling of responsibility for the boy stirred Brent and produced a new sensation which he puzzled over; for Brent was naturally carefree and, at times, cheerfully reckless.

Finally he gave up the idea of walking about the town, of indulging at cards or striking up a casual acquaintance with some man of the range, and went across to the hotel and up the stairs. To his surprise he passed Snally on the way, and the gambler gave no hint of recognition. Brent smiled to himself.

"Spiked his guns, whatever they were, anyway," he thought, and then his look froze.

Snag Dorgan was coming along the dimly lighted hall. He stopped before Brent with a gathering of his brows. But he spoke amiably enough.

"Was going out to look for you," he said. "Don't suppose you'd object to having a little talk after what you told Snally."

"That's accordin' to how you take what I told him," Brent answered.

"I take it well enough," said Dorgan, with a keen look. "I reckon you don't want any trouble on account of the kid, an' tipped me off. But I'd like to talk to you just the same."

"It's all right with me," Brent decided. "Where'll we talk?"

Dorgan turned and motioned to him to follow. Brent noted that Dorgan led the way to the room where he had seen the light. Dorgan turned the key in the lock and entered, walking directly to the table where he struck a match and lighted the lamp. He turned and looked sharply at Brent as the latter closed the door. Brent stood, returning the other's gaze steadily, and studying the man's face.

"Did you ever see me before our meeting to-day?" asked Dorgan.

Brent shook his head. "Not that I can remember."

"Then what makes you think you know who I really am?" demanded Dorgan.

"I've heard of you," replied Brent, with a frown.

"An' if I needed any proof that you were Snag Dorgan, Snally's look when I mentioned your name was enough."

"Snally's a fool!" blurted out Dorgan savagely.

"He's clever in a way," Brent drawled. "I'd say he was ahead of that man Royce."

This brought a sharper look from Dorgan. "You sure seem to be observing," he remarked. "But if you'd heard of me you must come from quite a ways south."

Brent shrugged. "I've traveled some," he said lightly, stepping nearer to the table.

Dorgan leaned toward him with his hands on the table. "Men from the south range don't usually hanker after this north country," he said slowly, keeping his eyes on Brent.

Brent's eyes widened. "That your opinion?" he said coolly.

"I know it to be a fact," replied Dorgan with a scowl. "Neither of us is up here for his health. I ain't a fool, an' I know a man who travels alone when I see him. You ain't had that youngster with you long. You'll probably drop him. You just naturally belong with a live outfit."

Brent looked at him for some time. "I reckon I ought to feel proud, eh, Dorgan? You're suggestin' that I should join up with you?"

The candid way Brent put the question caused Dorgan to lean back and look at him with new respect.

"I haven't said as much," he returned. "But I might be hittin' back south, an' you might be wanting to go that way. It ain't so lonesome, riding in pairs—south."

"I'm paired off now," said Brent cheerfully.

"With a kid!" exclaimed Dorgan. "You belong with men—with men who know the ropes, if I'm any judge. An' if you know anything about me, I guess you know I can handle the ropes." He stared at Brent meaningly. "Of course, if you've got to keep the kid . . ." He made a gesture that might have meant it would be all right with him.

Brent remained silent, eying Dorgan narrowly. It was an invitation to join with Dorgan. In what sort of a venture or ventures? He was tempted to find out. He felt a thrill at the prospect of excitement. Brent loved action. But he continued to withhold a reply to Dorgan's hints.

A sneer slowly formed on Dorgan's lips. "You ain't up to it?" he said.

"Up to what?" The question shot crisply from Brent, and Dorgan's eyes narrowed.

But Dorgan evidently had no idea of antagonizing his quarry. He succeeded in smiling and waving a hand in an apologetic gesture.

"Don't get riled," he soothed in a voice not altogether pleasant. "I ain't discounting a man from down my way." He nodded as though to assure Brent that it made little difference what Brent might know about him. "I ain't responsible for Royce's or Snally's actions. Both fools. Never mind about the hat. I reckon the kid's got spunk or you wouldn't be trailin' him along. Maybe you'll think over what I—didn't say in so many words, eh?"

"I think occasionally," said Brent coldly. He had a feeling that in some way he was tied down because of the boy. It irritated him before this man.

"I knew that," said Dorgan in a confidential tone. "An' I caught what you meant when you told Snally you didn't figure on makin' any announcements. A quiet tongue never got a man into trouble."

The two men looked at each other in understanding. But Brent continued to experience a nettled feeling that was close to chagrin. It vexed him, and when Dorgan smiled in a superior way he hated him for it on the instant. He turned toward the door.

"I'd be glad to see you when you're done thinking," said Dorgan.

Brent glimpsed a glitter in the man's small black eyes.

"I'm stayin' in town a day or two," Brent drawled out. "You'll probably get a chance to see me." His eyes narrowed and his hand dropped and caressed the butt of his gun.

"Forget the boy!" Dorgan said sharply as Brent went out.

CHAPTER SEVENTEEN
A Point Is Cleared

Brent and the boy were up at dawn next morning. When they had breakfasted they went out into the dazzling sunshine and proceeded directly to the barn to see that their horses were being well taken care of—a ceremony that Brent never neglected in town.

"Think of your hoss first, boy," he told Alan. "An' see that he knows you're thinkin' of him."

But the barn man had seen points in both horses that had impressed him, and he had taken excellent care of them. He grinned as Brent looked over his mount. The big-boned, dun-colored animal was anything but beautiful—looked, in fact, as if a ten-mile run would completely use him up, but the barn man's eyes twinkled as he met Brent's gaze.

"There's a horse I take it can travel," he said amiably. He had been impressed by Brent the afternoon before. Perhaps he associated the man with the horse as being both thoroughbreds.

"Maybe so," replied Brent laconically.

"You bet he can travel," Alan spoke up in a tone of pride. "He—" The boy ceased speaking as Brent nudged his arm and shot a look of warning.

Later, when they had saddled and mounted and

were riding on the plain west of town, Brent voiced his caution.

"It ain't a good plan, Alan, to boast about the merits of your hoss. Let the hoss show what he can do when he has to, an' then it may be that you'll be just as well satisfied that everybody didn't know what he could do in the first place."

He dwelt on this a little further until Alan knew exactly what he meant.

The boy, too, was mounted on a good horse. Brent had selected the best in the boy's father's string for the lad when his dead parent's stock was sold. It was a jet black gelding with a good head and chest and the legs of a race horse. And the boy could ride. Brent had discovered that before the trouble with the foreman cow thief—which had cost the boy's father his life and compelled Brent to protect his own by the rapidity of his draw.

They rode several miles west of town with the railroad north of them, and then turned south along a little creek and dismounted behind a screen of cottonwoods and willows. Here Alan indulged in more pistol practice, and under Brent's instruction showed more improvement. But Brent was careful to impress upon him the fact that he was teaching him to protect himself and not to acquire a skill to be used aggressively.

It was noon when they returned to town and put up the horses. After dinner Brent went for a walk, leaving the boy at the hotel. He took careful note of the buildings in the town, and at the east end of the street, beyond the large resort and the bank, he found a small house, set among some trees close to the stream. A card in a window bore the word: Rooms.

He ventured in, met the woman who ran the house, and engaged a room for himself and Alan at the rear of the second floor. Behind the house was a barn and a corral where they could keep their horses. That afternoon he and Alan left the hotel, saddled their horses with their belongings in the slicker packs behind, and rode by a round-about way to the house and took up their new quarters.

"We won't mention where we're living," he told the boy, "because there are no people in this town we have any business with—as yet. I don't take to livin' in that hotel with Snally an' that crowd aroun' so close."

"Are we goin' into Canada, Steve?" the boy asked eagerly.

Brent puckered his brow and then looked wistful. "Fall will be rompin' down on us before we know it, son, an' that country up there gets right cold, I've heard. No, I reckon we won't cross the line."

If Alan felt disappointed at this he failed to show it. His look showed plainly that any decision by Brent was satisfactory to him.

In selecting the house near the stream at the east

end of town, Brent made a happier choice than he at first suspected. They had arranged to get their meals at the house, and that night at supper discovered that the proprietress had a son about the same age as Alan. The two boys soon became acquainted, and Brent's problem as to what to do with the boy was solved. This left him free, for the time being, to follow his own bent.

This night Brent again sought the resort where he had seen Dorgan and the men with him. He saw Snally at cards, and Royce was playing, too. Dorgan was there, the center of a group, and, although he caught sight of Brent almost as soon as the latter entered, he gave no sign of recognition.

Brent sat in a game to while away a few hours and covertly to study the trio. This, however, got him nothing, for Snally played steadily with close attention to the game, Royce played casually, avoiding Brent's eyes, and Dorgan seemed strangely quiet. Snatches of the conversation informed Brent that Dorgan and the others with him were talking sheep.

He listened while he played, his back to the group, at a table near that where Snally and Royce sat. One fragment of conversation interested him particularly when he heard the Rabbit Butte country mentioned and heard Dorgan asking questions that seemed pertinent.

Brent frowned and thought to himself that

Dorgan appeared interested in what the others were saying. Brent's thoughts had repeatedly turned back to Rabbit Butte.

Dorgan and his companions left the place soon after this and Brent, finding himself but little concerned with the game, cashed his checks and went back to the house.

Next day Alan had another lesson in target hitting, and Brent saw that the boy was inclined to take naturally to the art of getting a gun into action with dispatch and shooting accurately. He suspected, also, that Alan would develop a knack of his own. He gave promise of this, and Brent reflected that it was such talent that made the expert. He stressed his point that the boy should always look upon his skill as a danger as well as an accomplishment.

On this day Brent saw nothing of Dorgan or the men with him. Nor did he see them the day following, which was Saturday. He assumed that they had left town, and while he did not lose a certain amount of interest in them and their movements, he decided it was just as well. Apparently Dorgan had come to the conclusion that it would be useless to attempt to form a connection with him. And Brent was seriously considering what he should do. It was the first time in his life that he found it necessary to think of someone other than himself. It was a new experience; it had its thrills and its draw-backs.

That night, leaving Alan with the boy at the house, Brent strolled aimlessly about the street. It was shortly before nine o'clock when he neared the house at the east end of town. Suddenly he heard shouts a short distance down the street. Then came the crash of guns.

Brent ran down the street, but he hadn't taken ten steps before he realized that the commotion was on the corner where the bank was situated. The shots ceased, but Brent could see the people near the corner running across the street. The shots evidently had frightened them away. The shouts continued. When Brent reached the corner, behind the bank, two men, with their faces masked, one of them carrying a bag, came around the building toward him, running. He swung in against the wall and dropped as shots rang out and bullets whistled over his head and spattered against the wall.

His own gun leaped into his hand as the men dashed across the street to the shelter of the trees which extended to the house near the stream. But he held his fire for a space, and in this interval—a matter of split seconds—the men disappeared in the shadows.

His first thought was one of wonder, If the bank bandits had wished to shoot him down they could have done so, in his opinion. But he had scant time for reflection.

Men came running down the street as crowds

poured out of the various buildings to see what was the matter. Then one of the bank officials appeared in his shirt sleeves, gesticulating wildly.

"They've robbed the bank!"

The cry went up from a hundred throats. There was no need for the bank official to shout what had happened. Men came in crowds until the space in front of the building was densely packed.

Brent edged through the throng to where he could see the bank entrance.

"Anybody hurt?" a man called loudly, forcing his way through to the steps.

Brent caught the gleam of the lamps on a silver star and smiled grimly. The bank official shook his head and continued to wave his arms and point in all directions. He was too excited to speak.

"How much did they get?" shouted the man of authority, shaking the official by the arm.

Still the man remained inarticulate, and the officer led him inside.

Brent turned away and slipped through the crowd to the street leading to the house. He realized that it would be some time before the extent of the loot could be ascertained. But, with hundreds of laborers depositing a portion of their wages on this Saturday night, and with the bank having a large amount of cash available to cash pay checks, it was certain that the loss would be substantial. And, so far as he knew, he was the only one near who had noticed for a certainty the direction the bandits had taken in escaping. By now they were doubtless out on the prairie, riding hard.

He paused, thought for a few moments, and then turned back down the strect.

CHAPTER EIGHTEEN
Queer Moves

When Brent reached the packed space in front of the bank and succeeded in pushing his way to a spot where he could see the entrance, the officer, whom he assumed to be the sheriff, came out on the steps and held up an arm to still the babble of voices.

"Give the sheriff a chance to talk!" someone in the crowd shouted.

In a few moments there was a hush of expectancy. Through the windows of the bank behind the officer, Brent could see the bank officials in conference in one of the front cages. They were evidently making a hurried attempt to estimate the loss. One of them called to the sheriff, and the latter turned back into the bank for a moment. When he again came out and faced the crowd there was no need to call for quiet.

"Men, the bank has been robbed of a big sum of money by two masked bandits," the sheriff said loudly. "The bank offers a reward of three thousand dollars for their capture, and I offer two thousand more on behalf of the county. I want every man who has a horse and a gun ready to start after them in fifteen minutes or sooner. We'll meet in front of the hotel."

He hurried down from the steps, waving the crowd away, while the bank doors were closed by someone inside.

The crowd broke up rapidly. Cow-punchers and others, eager to join the posses and with minds inflamed by the prospects of sharing in the rewards, ran to get their horses. Laborers and others gathered in the street in groups, talking excitedly.

Brent remained in the background. The grim smile, hinting of sarcasm, still played upon his lips. In his own mind the point proven by the hold-up of the bank was that Snag Dorgan and his two companions had played their trump card in Shelton. They had left town to quiet suspicion, had ridden in by way of the stream, screened by the trees and willows, and had left the same way. In the fleeting seconds when he had glimpsed the masked men running across the street, after they had fired at him, he had noted that one of them was a big man and that the other was nearly as large. The big man had carried the sack containing the plunder. It was not difficult to conjecture that this pair were Dorgan and Royce. Snally doubtless had attended to the horses in the shadow of the trees. And now the trio had nearly half an hour of a start.

Brent's smile faded as he considered the boldness of the robbery. It was, according to what he had heard in that south country from which he hailed, a typical Dorgan holdup. He pressed his lips tightly as he recalled the shots fired at him. Had they recognized him and shot merely to stop him, with no intention of hitting him? He reflected that Dorgan, bad as he was, might do this out of consideration for his, Brent's silence regarding his identity. But he did not believe Royce would overlook an opportunity to shoot him dead if he could safely do so. The next moment Brent remembered something else he had heard of Dorgan. The man had been careful not to deal death in the course of his depredations. He had killed men, yes; but he had always provoked the draw, beaten the other man to it, and thus been able to claim that he fired in self-defense. Dorgan was clever.

Brent mingled with the crowds near the hotel. The shrill whistle of a locomotive was heard, repeating itself in a series of long blasts. The sheriff appeared in a growing group of horsemen in the space before the hotel. He dismounted at the hotel steps, leaped to the porch, and gestured to the crowd for silence.

"We're sending a train north as far as the line is built," he shouted. "We want a bunch of men to go up there and spread out in case these robbers try to make the line by the wagon roads. We're sending horses, too. Those of you who want to go, get over to the station."

Brent edged back through the crowd, restraining

a laugh. The sheriff was evidently convinced that the bandits would make for Canada. And the official's slowness to take up the pursuit, his methods, and even his talk impressed Brent as amateurish in a marked degree. This official was doubtless a political sheriff, he thought to himself; not much like the man who wore the derby and enforced the law down Rabbit Butte way.

Brent stopped in his tracks, and his brow knitted. He remembered the scraps of information he had obtained from the conversation of Dorgan and the others in the resort some nights before. It suddenly struck him that Dorgan couldn't very well take him in on a play like the one that had been staged this night if he had insisted on having the boy along. Alan would be a hindrance.

He hurried on past the bank, where lights still gleamed in the house where he was staying. Alan and the other boy were up, talking excitedly with the woman of the house; for the news of the hold-up had spread rapidly. He ordered Alan to bed, spoke a few words to the landlady, and himself sought a couch in their room where he lay down with his clothes on. He knew by the boy's restlessness that the youngster wouldn't sleep much. He woke him before dawn, and they crept downstairs, carrying their few belongings.

The landlady was making coffee and preparing breakfast for them in the kitchen, and they went out and saddled their horses. When they returned breakfast was ready. They ate, Brent paid the score, and they were soon in their saddles.

Brent led the way south, following the stream to where it turned east, and then leaving it for the open prairie. It was still dark, and Alan could not see his face distinctly. If he wondered at Brent's move, he did not voice his perplexity in questions. Nor did Brent do any talking. Had the boy been able to look into his eyes, he would have seen that they were troubled, and he would have noticed that Brent bit his lips as though he struggled with wavering decisions and doubts. But his attitude in general was determined enough.

The gray light of dawn appeared in the east, brightened gradually, disclosing the great sweep of prairie to southward and the towering hulks of the mountains above the foothills to westward, and then the sun came up.

Alan looked at Brent and smiled without comment. From time to time Brent turned or rose slightly in his saddle for a look around. Then they spied the entrance to the coulee, where the trees grew about the spring where they had stopped for lunch on their way into Shelton.

Brent headed for it, and soon they swung down the defile to the wide space about the spring. Brent dismounted hurriedly and looked keenly at the ground.

"I thought so," he said finally, straightening.

He pointed to fresh tracks of horses' hoofs in the gumbo and soft turf. "Dorgan's no fool," he muttered. "He headed straight for the spring, knowin' he could get out of here at the lower end an' swing up an' around 'em if they came in in the night. Sometimes you can fool a posse by stayin' close to it," he said to Alan with a wink.

"You talkin' about the robbers?" asked the boy eagerly.

"I—think so," said Brent. "I'm goin' to take a look."

He mounted and rode about the lower end of the coulee and up to the flat ground above it. There he motioned to the boy to join him.

"Know anything about the country west of here?" he asked, his eyes on the imprints of hoofs leading westward.

The boy hesitated, looking at the foothills. Then he shook his head.

"But Freezeout Bench is down south of here among the foothills north of Rabbit Butte," he said. "It's hard to get on and off Freezeout, an' there ain't a thing on it hardly but there's ten miles straight that's smooth as a race track. Dad used to say many a rustler got up there where the goin' was good an' leave the men who were after him behind in a race for the other end."

"But Freezeout Bench wouldn't make a good hidin' place," Brent mused. "We'll go west," he added, looking again at the tracks.

They rode on at a canter, and hadn't proceeded two miles before Brent caught sight of horsemen bearing down from the northwest foothills. He spurred his horse, with a shout to the boy to follow.

CHAPTER NINETEEN
Horseflesh

Brent and Alan rode due west for two miles or so. Brent was setting a fast pace, but he was not exerting his horse nor that of the boy. Meanwhile, the riders to the northwest of them had seen them and were coming like the wind. Brent kept an eye on them and, leaning over his horse's neck, strained to keep the tracks of the earlier riders in view.

He already had ascertained that there were three sets of tracks; that three men had ridden that way during the night or early in the morning before dawn. He believed the three mysterious horsemen to be Dorgan, Royce, and Snally; was convinced they had fled that way after holding up the bank at Shelton. And he knew the riders bearing down from the northwest were members of a posse that had been sent in that direction.

But Brent apparently had no idea of stopping for a conference with the posse, which would involve their questioning as to why he had left town so early, where he was going, who he was, and all that. He knew, too, that the deputy in charge of the posse would want to know why he had not joined with the pursuers the night before. There might be other questions and answering them would take time, and it was not at all certain that he and Alan would not be sent back to Shelton to await the return of the sheriff, who more than likely had gone north where he thought the bank robbers had fled.

Brent looked around at the boy. Alan was riding alongside him, his face flushed with excitement, his eyes sparkling and eager. Brent noted something that had escaped his attention, and a surprised look came into his eyes. When he looked ahead again, he grinned. The boy was wearing his gun belt with its worn holster containing his weapon. Brent sobered quickly and looked at the lad, who met his gaze serenely. It seemed to Brent that Alan had stepped from mere boyhood into young manhood overnight. It rather startled him. But Alan was larger and more experienced than the average boy of his age. Also, he appeared more ambitious.

It was still several miles to the foothills, and Brent soon saw that the approaching riders stood to head them off if they were to continue straight ahead toward the hills. In fact, coming as they were from the northwest, they were more than likely to cut Brent and the boy off from the hills and compel them to ride south on the prairie. Brent frowned at the thought, for he wished to lose the posse entirely.

He changed their course to the southwest and urged the lanky dun into a faster pace. A streamer of dust trailed behind the riders to northward. It was plain to see that they were mounted on horses to be reckoned with. Brent kept a keen eye on them and came to the conclusion that they, too, were saving their horses. They could not be expected to know that more than two men were concerned in the hold-up, and in Brent and the boy they saw two men. Furthermore, if they were undecided, Brent's action in running from them would appear conclusive proof that they were on the right trail.

All this Brent took into consideration as they sped into the southwest, still with the foothills ahead of them, but farther away. He kept throwing glances at the boy, and to all appearances was wrestling with the problems that had been tormenting him for days. He could not analyze these, exactly, but they concerned his future and Alan's to no uncertain extent. In fact, Steve Brent was wondering if it wouldn't be better to leave the boy in some town, making provision for his keep, and go his way on the long trails of adventure alone, as he had in the past.

He saw the boy pointing, and rode in closer to him.

"Freezeout Bench starts down there," cried the boy.

Alan was trying to give his protector all the knowledge he possessed of the country north of Rabbit Butte, where he had lived so many years.

Brent nodded, and his gaze roved into the southeast. The foothills jogged out into the prairie for a few miles down there, clothed with a growth of jack pine, buck brush, and cedar bushes. Somewhere below them Brent knew the bad lands began and stretched southward to Rabbit Butte. This bad-land district would furnish a natural hiding place for fugitives. Brent felt that he was pretty well acquainted with the southern portion of the district, but of the northern half he knew nothing.

He looked behind and turned his head quickly, with the knowledge that the pursuing riders had indulged in a spurt and lessened the gap between them.

"We'll make for Freezeout!" he shouted to the boy, above the pound of hoofs. "Lead the way, now, an' slope!"

Alan drove his spurs into the flanks of his big black, and they struck a pace that caused Brent to open his eyes and momentarily left him behind. But the dun was not accustomed to eating dust, and quickly made up the lost ground.

Brent's eyes sparkled in admiration as he watched the boy in his saddle. Alan rode as if he had been born to it, which was, indeed, the case.

The green of the foothills seemed rushing toward them. Faint openings began to show in the band of green, marking entrances into the tumbled country ahead. Behind them, the dust streamer trailing above their pursuers became a cloud. The boy saw this, too, and cried out in excitement. He did not know why Brent wished to run away from the horsemen behind them, but it was enough that he wished to do so. He spurred his horse to ever greater efforts and brought a look of genuine astonishment to Brent's face.

The dun extended himself a bit, the green band ahead dissolved into the irregular contour of the hills, and an open space, wider than the rest, loomed straight in their path. The foothills extended some distance in the east now, and both parties of riders were racing due south. It seemed as though they covered the intervening distance to the opening in seconds instead of minutes, and before they realized it, their horses dashed into a long ravine.

Alan checked the speed of his mount and looked askance at Brent. He received a nod from Brent, approving his saving of the horse's powers of endurance. The ravine had an upward slope, narrowed gradually, and soon they were on a thin trail that curled about a ridge and finally surmounted it. From the crest Brent saw ahead what appeared to be a long, low butte with steep sides. A light streak against its dark slope, which showed above the trees, suggested a trail.

"That's Freezeout," called the boy, pointing.

Brent waved him on, and they proceeded down the south side of the ridge into the timber.

The trail led through coulees and ravines, across gravel patches and stretches of gumbo and alkali not unlike those which are characteristic of the bad lands.

Finally they emerged upon a hard bit of trail that led up a steep slope. Brent recognized the north side of the bench called Freezeout. He looked behind as they neared the top, and saw their pursuers on the crest of the ridge they had left a few minutes before.

A chorus of yells came to their ears. They could see the members of the posse distinctly. The men were waving to them to stop. Then guns came up and shots rang on the air. Bullets whined past Brent and the boy as they swung over the shoulder of the bench and started south upon it, losing sight of the posse.

Brent soon realized why it was called Freezeout Bench. It was as smooth as a table top, almost, and nearly bare. The wind whistled across it, and it was easy to imagine it a sea of swirling white in a blizzard in the winter. Even in the summer it was cool, forbidding. And it was as level as it is possible for land to be.

After a look at the long, smooth stretch ahead, Brent drew a long breath.

"This is where we leave 'em," he muttered to himself.

He leaned over the dun's neck and seemed to whisper in the horse's ear as he tickled the animal with his spurs. The dun shot ahead with the black following. Faster and faster ran the horses, almost neck and neck. Brent shifted his weight to the left side of his saddle and looked back over his right shoulder. It was not long before he saw the posse gain the top of the bench and start after them. He counted six men. Then he turned his attention to the vista ahead.

The boy had said the bench was ten miles long. Brent quickly computed distances and decided that the northern edge of the bad lands above Rabbit Butte was just below the southern end of Freezeout. He leaned forward in his saddle, spoke sharply to the dun, and punctuated his verbal entreaty with a dig of his spurs.

The dun leaped ahead, increasing his speed when it would have seemed to an onlooker that such a thing would be impossible. In a moment the black was extending itself to the utmost, running, as Brent suspected, faster than it had ever run before. The ground flew under them, the floor of the bench was a streak of gray, the green of the timber on the hills to westward became a blur.

Alan rode as if he was glued to the saddle. Brent looked at him in frank admiration. It was the pretty performance of a natural-born horseman —dear to the heart of the range rider. Brent held the dun in just enough to allow the black to keep up with him. Indeed, the dun could have made but a fraction of greater speed. Brent suspected that the black would become as fast a horse as his own after he had been paced on a few occasions and had gotten in better trim.

A look behind showed that Brent and Alan were rapidly leaving the posse behind. There were no more shots. It was plain, too, that the pursuers were spurring their horses at top speed. But they lost rapidly, and Brent smiled with the thought that the horses of the posse had likely been in the barns in town for days, and were soft.

As they left the posse farther and farther behind, Brent gradually slowed the pace. It seemed incredible that they had covered more than half the distance across the bench and had left their pursuers fully two miles behind in the spurt, but Brent saw that this was the truth. He could descry the tangled tree growth of the bad lands to southward. He kept the pace at a heartbreaking point for another mile and then eased his mount. The pursuers were losing steadily.

Alan's face was shining with joyous exhilaration. He rode straight in the saddle now, with his right hand resting lightly on the butt of his gun.

"Where we goin' from here, Steve?" he called when Brent next looked at him.

"Do you know the bad-land country up here?" Brent asked.

The boy nodded soberly.

"Then we'll lose 'em when we get down off the bench," said Brent.

Shortly afterward they reined in at the southern end of the long bare strip of table-land. The posse was half the distance of the bench behind, almost.

"Go ahead," Brent directed the boy.

Alan pushed in front and led the way down the steep trail from the bench. When he gained the timber in the bottom he turned sharply to the left and sent his horse through a screen of bushes, with Brent following closely. They came into a deep gully or wash with a gravel bottom, veered to the south, and went clattering down the wash to gain a dim trail leading southeast through the timber. Presently they came to a small stream, and the boy followed this for a time, turned into a trail starting on a series of flat rocks and wound about a steep ridge. Before they gained the top of the ridge the boy left the trail and plunged through the bushes and down the slope, his horse and that of Brent sliding and slipping, and thus came into a ravine thick with cottonwoods and poplars.

Brent was impressed with Alan's instinct for leaving a blind trail. The boy knew how to follow a given direction without sighting from a ridge. He had avoided the crest of the ridge so they wouldn't be seen by the men who were following and who probably had reached the high point at the end of the bench. This natural talent for the trail increased Brent's respect for the lad.

Alan led the way into another dim trail at the

end of the ravine, and in a short time they rode into a little open space, where he reined in his mount and looked at Brent questioningly.

Brent stroked the neck of his sweating horse and then rolled a cigarette.

"You know the way to the cabin from here, of course," he observed when he had lighted his smoke.

"We can get there in an hour and a half," the boy assured him.

Brent saw that the boy was concerned, that he wanted to ask questions; for Brent referred to the cabin where the boy had lived with his father. But Brent was in no mood for answering questions nor for making explanations. He looked up at the sun, now high in the sky, pinched out the light in his cigarette, tossed the weed away, and nodded to the boy to proceed.

They now followed a definite system of trails in the labyrinth of the bad lands. They heard nothing of their pursuers. In less than two hours they saw a large clearing ahead through the interlacing branches, and a spiral of smoke curling above the trees.

The boy drew rein quickly and looked at Brent in surprise. But Brent did not appear disturbed. He dismounted leisurely and motioned to the lad to follow his example.

"Wait here with the horses," he instructed. "I'm goin' to see who's in your cabin."

He walked along the trail without looking back, stepped into the clearing, and strode toward the cabin, from the chimney of which the smoke spiral issued.

CHAPTER TWENTY
Two Kinds of Talk

As he proceeded across the clearing Brent noted that three horses were grazing in the big meadow beyond the cabin. He recognized them and saw three saddles hanging from posts of the corral behind the cabin. There was no evidence that whoever might be in the cabin had but lately arrived, or that any hurried attempt might be made to leave.

This puzzled him. Was Dorgan so certain he hadn't been followed there? It was possible. Surely the men from the north were not familiar with the bad-land country in there or knew of the location of the cabin. Dorgan had undoubtedly secured his information regarding the place from someone in Shelton the night Brent had heard parts of the conversation in the resort. But the trio had been careful to give the impression that they had left town, and it was not likely that whoever had given this information would, on the spur of the moment, recollect and direct suspicion toward them and acquaint the sheriff with the facts regarding that talk. If such had been the case the sheriff would have sent a sizable force to the spot at once. Dorgan certainly hadn't expected pursuit there. And it had been Brent who had led the posse in that direction.

Before Brent reached the open door of the cabin a man stepped out and stood looking at him, waiting with his hands on his hips, bareheaded.

It was Snag Dorgan.

As Brent came up a shrewd gleam came into Dorgan's eyes, and he grinned. The grin, however, changed to a sneer as he spoke.

"Finish your thinking?" he asked.

"I sure did, Dorgan! An' now it's up to you to do some." Brent saw both Snally and Royce appear in the doorway behind their leader.

"I'm capable of it," said Dorgan, with a frown. "Let's have it as fast as you can talk. Where's your horse?" he added suspiciously.

"Better hid than yours," Brent answered. "You'd be hard put to make a quick get-away."

Dorgan's eyes narrowed, but his voice was smooth as silk. "Hadn't thought about movin' fast. You drop in to give us a few pointers?"

Royce laughed, while Snally looked at Brent searchingly.

"I dropped in to give you a tip," said Brent. "There's half a dozen hard-ridin', easy-shootin' gents combing their way down through the brakes toward this place."

"So?" Dorgan's look belied his tone of indifference. "You bring 'em down?"

"They took after me an' I didn't feel like havin' a powwow," said Brent. "I ran away from 'em, but

178

the last I saw of 'em they acted like they wasn't intending to quit the chase."

"Oh, well, if they come along here, we won't mention seeing you," said Dorgan brazenly. "Where's the kid? You been cuttin' loose an'—"

"Drop it!" said Brent sharply. "You saw enough in me to bait me with a proposition, Dorgan; now put two an' two together an' give me credit for bein' able to do the same thing. You did some mighty poor shootin'—last night."

Dorgan looked at him steadily. "Is that what sent you down here?"

The cool, indirect admission of his knowledge of the events of the night before showed Dorgan to be fearless as well as daring. Snally and Royce now were listening breathlessly.

"There's a heap of reward money up for certain parties that turned a trick in Shelton last night," said Brent slowly. "But I don't know as the hard-ridin' gents up the way have any idea who they're lookin' for."

"Did they get a look at you?" asked Dorgan quickly.

"They saw somebody ridin' ahead of 'em, that's all."

"Money's a nice thing to have," said Dorgan, sneering again. "That's what set you thinking?"

"If it was, I wouldn't be here alone," Brent replied. "I know too much about you, Dorgan, to think you'd cut me in on anything. You can figure out my play for yourself, but I've given you a straight tip about the gents that are easin' their way down here." He swung on his heel and stepped away.

"Wait a minute!" Dorgan's words came in a tone of command.

Brent stopped and half turned as Dorgan strode up to him.

"You're not a fool," said Dorgan in a low voice. "You had some other reason for coming down here besides tipping me off, as you say. You can play any kind of a game with me you want—so long as I know what it is. You couldn't have tracked us in here, an' I know there wasn't anybody near us this morning. You say I did some poor shooting last night? If I did I can tell you there's times I shoot better. What brought you here? How'd you know we were here?"

The man's eyes were darting beads of menace; his voice had changed from a whisper to a hiss; he was in deadly earnest.

Brent's brows went up as he looked at the other coolly.

"I didn't know you were here. You found this place had been lived in, didn't you? It was here, right in that cabin, that I got that boy, Dorgan. His father was shot for keeps in there. I've been here before. We—the boy an' I—may want to hang up here for a spell. The place still belongs to him. If you figure I've got any good reason to lie to you, a few inquiries at the Rabbit Foot Ranch below the butte south of here will put you right. They know the story."

"A man can tell the truth an' still lie," said Dorgan, half convinced.

"That's beyond my education," said Brent crisply.

"The boy with you?" demanded Dorgan.

"He is," replied Brent after a moment of hesitation.

Dorgan pursed his lips thoughtfully. Then he laughed.

"The place is yours," he said with a mock bow. "But if this is a game, it's your move."

He turned back to the cabin and Brent walked across the clearing to the trail where he had left Alan with the horses. A few minutes later the thunder of hoofs came from the clearing, and they saw Dorgan and the two others riding away on the trail leading from the south end of the meadow beyond the cabin.

Alan's eyes were wide with wonder. "How'd they get here?" he asked. "Did you know they were here, Steve?"

"I wasn't sure of it," grumbled Brent as much to himself as in reply to the boy's question. "He said I couldn't have tracked 'em in, an' I showed him I knew this country in here an' that you used to live here. That's enough for him. An' I didn't lie in telling him the truth about that." He stood thoughtfully. "But a man hasn't got to tell all he knows or thinks unless he's so minded, I reckon," he added grimly.

"Steve!" Alan breathed the word in soft exclamation. "Did they—did they rob the bank?"

This brought Brent up sharply. "You're an observin' little cuss," he said. "What makes you think that?"

"Because we left town so early," replied the boy earnestly. "An' you picked up tracks that started us west. Then we ran away from those men up there. We found Dorgan and those two here. You didn't seem surprised, Steve. An' now they've gone after—after you—"

The boy paused, with a startled look in his eyes. Brent read his thought.

"Don't worry, son, we're not in on the swag the hold-ups got," he said, putting a hand on the boy's shoulder. "All I had to do with that business up there was to get a hunch. I'm playin' it—that hunch. I'm a hand to play hunches, Alan. You can help the play by forgettin' to talk, see?"

The boy's face had brightened as Brent talked. He grasped the older man's arm. "We're pardners, ain't we, Steve?" he said soberly.

"Danged if I don't believe we are!" Brent ejaculated. "Let's go to the cabin."

They mounted and rode to the corral where they unsaddled and turned the horses out to graze on the luscious grass in the meadow. Then they went into the cabin. The fire was still burning in the stove, and there was hot water. When Brent and Alan had left the place after Alan's father's death, they had left some provisions. These were untouched, save for a small amount Dorgan and the others had used that morning, and Alan at once began to prepare a meal.

After they had eaten, Brent suggested to the boy that he get a little rest. But Alan scorned this advice. He insisted upon another lesson with his gun, and Brent granted the request. Afterward Alan practiced for some time. He was shooting from the hip now, and Brent watched him with conflicting emotions of pride and doubt. It was a foregone conclusion that the boy was destined by natural talent to become a gun expert of the most proficient kind.

In mid-afternoon six horsemen rode into the clearing while Brent and the boy were standing talking in the meadow. The riders swooped down upon them with guns drawn.

Alan looked at Brent in dismay. "They heard my shooting!" he said in a tone of self-reproach. "I brought 'em!"

"What of it?" said Brent, and then looked up at the leader of the posse, who was covering him.

"Put 'em up!" ordered the leader sternly.

"No need for that, Mr. Deputy," said Brent coolly. "There's six of you gents." He made no move to comply with the demand.

"Keep him covered," said the deputy briskly to his companions. Then he dismounted, after a long look at the two horses grazing nearby.

"Looks like you've been ridin' some by the sweat streaks on those horses," he said to Brent.

"We have," Brent replied readily. "We've come all the way from Shelton since mornin'."

The deputy seemed taken aback. He glared at Brent as he spoke again.

"Didn't seem to want to see us very much, the way you lit out up there," he said pointedly.

"Oh, was that you?" drawled out Brent, lifting his brows. "I hadn't left word for any messengers to follow us, an' our hosses needed exercising."

"You're cool enough," said the deputy angrily. "You thought you could lose us, an' I guess you've had time to stow away the loot. But you'll have a hard time explaining things to the sheriff an' the judge in Shelton."

"Looks bad, doesn't it?" observed Brent. "Bank is robbed an' the two of us light right out of town before daylight. Course the boy, here, is a little young, but he's big as lots of men, an' with a mask on he might help me to hold up a bank by scaring the audience away with a few shots. Yes, it looks bad—plumb ornery. An' with us leavin' you behind that way." He shook his head dubiously.

The deputy was puzzled as well as angry. But he saw a germ of what could easily be the truth in Brent's speech.

"I ain't asking you to talk," he snapped out. "But I'll have to ask you to kindly accompany us back to Shelton." There was mock politeness in his speech.

"That can't be unreasonable," said Brent. "But our hosses won't stand the trip to-day, an' neither will yours. There ain't any place much here to stay, but there's a town—the county seat of this county—a few miles southeast of here, where they have eatin' places an' beds, a sheriff, an' a jail. Suppose we go down there before we start back."

The deputy looked around and saw looks of approval on the faces of his posse. After the long hard ride, the prospect of good food and beds was pleasant. The mention of the sheriff and jail assured the safe-keeping of the prisoners.

"We'll do that," said the deputy shortly. "I'll have to ask you for your guns."

"Shore," said Brent heartily. He drew his weapon from its holster and handed it over. Alan, astonished, followed his example.

"Now you can saddle up an' we'll be starting," said the deputy. He turned to his men. "Two of you watch 'em," he instructed. "Might search 'em, too. The rest of us will go through the place an' see what we can find. I don't expect to find much, though, for this is about the smoothest piece of work I ever heard of!"

Brent laughed softly. There was something in

that laugh that irritated the deputy as well as puzzled him.

"Thanks," Brent drawled out. "I reckon your fast ride has just naturally made you keener than a Mexican's knife, Deputy."

"Saddle up!" commanded the deputy, enraged.

An hour later, after a fruitless search of the cabin and premises, the little cavalcade rode out of the bad lands east of the clearing and struck across the open prairie toward town.

CHAPTER TWENTY-ONE
In and Out

Sheriff Ed Furness sat in his little office in the diminutive county jail. It was nine o'clock in the evening, and the lamp shed a yellow glow over the paper he was reading. His feet were cocked on his desk, and his derby hat was pushed far back on his head. He did not look up from his paper as there came a shuffle of boots on the steps outside and a number of men came stamping into the office.

When he peered languidly over the top of the paper he saw Steve Brent and Alan Carman standing before his desk, surrounded by half a dozen others. He put down the paper, but did not change his position.

"You the sheriff?" asked one of the men, stepping forward.

"Yes," was the drawling reply. "I'm the sheriff."

"I'm Deputy Smith from Shelton," said the spokesman. "I've got two prisoners here to leave till morning."

Furness eyed him thoughtfully. "You a new man up there?" he asked.

"Yes—that is—I'm not exactly new," replied the deputy. "I've been on for six months."

"I see," returned Furness, stroking his mustaches. "I've been here about sixteen years an' know most of the deputies from other counties in the north country, but I hadn't seen you. Where's the prisoners?"

"Why, here," was the surprised reply. "This man an' this youngster," he added, pointing to Brent and Alan.

Sheriff Furness looked at them. Brent was nonchalantly rolling a cigarette, and there was a faint smile on Alan's lips. Furness knew them both. He hadn't forgotten the good work Brent had done, on his own initiative, in breaking up the band of rustlers who had been stealing cattle. But, even at that, he had never quite understood Brent, knew nothing of his past; and he had to confess to himself that he never had been absolutely sure of him.

"Who are they?" he inquired mildly.

"The man says his name is Brent an' the boy is supposed to be an Alan Carman, or something like that," replied the deputy, vexed at the sheriff's manner. "I expect the names don't mean any-thing."

"Maybe not," said Furness, taking his feet off the desk and tipping his derby hat over his right eye.

"I've heard of you," said Smith. "Your derby hat is famous in this country." There was a subtle hint of derision in his tone.

"It isn't a bad hat," said Furness. "Suits me."
He drew a paper from a drawer of his desk.

"What's the charge?" he asked calmly.

"Why—er—there ain't any definite charge yet," stammered Smith. "But I don't have to make a charge here," he continued in a louder voice. "I've arrested this pair on suspicion of having held up the bank at Shelton last night an' got away with several thousand dollars."

"Oh—then you're not sure you really have the right parties?" asked Furness mildly.

"I'm sure they can't give a satisfactory explanation of why they beat it out of Shelton before daybreak, an'—"

"Did you see us go?" Brent interrupted.

Smith turned on him angrily. "I saw you about as soon as the sun was up, an' you had to leave town a long time before that to get where you were. I know that, an' I know what time we left."

Brent waved his cigarette in the air and nodded at Sheriff Furness.

"We left early," he confessed. "We had quite a way to go."

"You hear that!" cried Smith. "An' when they saw us they sloped as fast as their horses could go; hid in the rough country south of that long bench northwest of here."

"Freezeout Bench," said Brent, nodding again. "They found us in a cabin in the bad lands north of Rabbit Butte. Both of us had been there before."

"I see," said Sheriff Furness gravely. "Did you find the money on them, Smith?"

"He's too smart for that," replied the deputy, turning an accusing gaze on Brent. "I haven't had time to investigate everything yet; but I've got enough to hold him."

There was a murmur of approval from the men with the deputy.

"I suppose a reward has been offered," the sheriff remarked dryly.

"Five thousand, so far," said Smith, with a look around.

"There must have been more than several thousand stolen," Furness observed.

"I don't know how much was taken," said Smith impatiently. "They hadn't figured it up yet when we left. But it was plenty, you can lay to that."

The sheriff had been glancing now and then at Brent, and Brent had met his gaze each time.

"You want to keep them here to-night?" the sheriff said to Smith. "That's what you want?"

"Exactly. You're the sheriff of the county, an' this is the jail. Our horses are too much done up to go on north to-night. So I brought my prisoners in here for safe-keeping. I want 'em jailed." There was both sarcasm and determination in the deputy's tone.

The sheriff pushed the paper on his desk aside, took out a huge key from a drawer, rose, and started for the door leading into the rear portion of the jail building.

Brent and the boy followed, with Smith and the others close behind them. The jail room contained three cells. The sheriff swung open the door of the center cell and motioned to Brent and Alan to enter. When they were inside he locked the door and peered in at them through the bars. A single lamp in a bracket on the wall shed a faint, yellow light on the faces of the prisoners.

"You agree to stay in town to-night?" the sheriff asked.

Smith and the others laughed as Brent nodded.

"That wasn't a bad joke, Sheriff," said Smith with a swagger as they went back into the office. "Maybe that's why you wear a derby hat. Maybe you're a humorist."

"Maybe I am," drawled out the sheriff. "I hadn't thought of that."

Brent looked at the anxious face of the boy and smiled broadly as the words came to his ears.

Then they heard the members of the posse going out the front door.

Brent sat down on one of the bunks and Alan sat on the other. The boy seemed awed, interested, rather than frightened, and he looked at Brent trustingly.

Brent rolled a cigarette and lighted it. He gazed at Alan speculatively.

"This is what men get when they rob banks or get too free with their guns, son," he said slowly. "If you should ever get it into your head that you want to hit the wrong trail, remember those." He pointed to the bars and the pattern they made on the floor of the cell in the dim light of the lamp.

Alan looked, and his eyes met Brent's with a gleam of understanding.

"They've got us both in jail, pardner," he said in a low voice, with a queer smile.

"Dog-gone if you ain't got a sense of humor!" Brent exclaimed. Then he laughed heartily.

Sheriff Furness appeared in the doorway leading to the cells.

"What you laughing at?" he inquired, toying with his mustaches.

"I'm laughing at that joke of yours," replied Brent, chuckling. "I always thought you wore a derby for some good reason, Sheriff."

Furness scowled. "Did you run away from that outfit?" he demanded.

"We shore did, Ed. We shore left 'em with the berry pickers. It was a great mornin' for ridin'."

The sheriff eyed him keenly. "What time did the hold-up come off?"

"Round nine o'clock last night."

"You started out early?"

"Somewhere round four, I guess. Wanted to give the boy here a chance to get some sleep."

"Have any particular reason for lighting out so early?" asked Furness in a casual tone. He kept his eyes on Brent's.

Brent shrugged. "I usually have a reason for what I do in my simple-minded way," he drawled out.

"Did you go to bed last night same time as the boy?" asked Furness.

"Same time. 'Bout ten I guess it was—wasn't it, Alan?"

"Five minutes to ten," the boy responded. "He didn't have a thing to do with the robbery, Sheriff."

"He wasn't askin' you anything, Alan," Brent reproved him.

The boy had risen, but now he sank back on the bunk, crestfallen. The sheriff looked at him intently for the first time.

"Seems older than when he left here," he commented. He looked again at Brent. "Anything you want?"

"I'm just tryin' to think when was the last time we ate," said Brent.

Sheriff Furness stepped to the door of the cell, unlocked it, and swung it open. Brent walked out, followed by the boy, whose eyes were bulging.

"You better get some supper," said the sheriff, leading the way into his office and dropping into his chair.

"Any particular time you expect us back?" asked Brent, looking at his gun, which was lying, with Alan's, on the sheriff's desk.

"Expect Smith will be around looking for you early in the morning," Furness answered. "Which of those is your gun?"

Brent picked up his weapon and slipped it into its holster.

"See you later, Sheriff," he said, motioning to the boy.

He opened the door and the two of them stepped out into the street.

CHAPTER TWENTY-TWO
Three Meetings

Rangeview, as is characteristic of old cow towns off the railroads, boasted few real eating places. Stockmen and punchers patronized the hotel for a square meal and at other times depended upon the lunch counters in the various resorts or the small "short-order" cafés. Brent chose one of the latter for the very good reason that the hotel dining room was closed at that hour.

They perched on adjoining stools and ordered ham and eggs, fried potatoes, pie, and coffee.

Brent looked at Alan's joyous face and said, with a twinkle in his eye: "We haven't eaten in jail yet!"

This brought a laugh from Alan, who did not understand how they had come to get out, but who was content to let events take their course. Before the food arrived, however, he leaned toward Brent and whispered in his ear.

"Do we have to sleep there to-night?"

"You won't," said Brent with a smile. "But it's beginning to look to me as if I might have to do some tall thinkin' an' sleuthing to keep out long myself." He was half serious in this, but he laughed softly when he saw the boy's look of concern.

"There's one thing you've got to learn, Alan, if you're goin' to travel with me," he told the boy. "You've got to learn not to worry."

"I don't like that Smith," said Alan irrelevantly.

"I don't reckon me or the sheriff's in love with him either," observed Brent with a chuckle. "Here's the grub."

After the meal they strolled down the street. The excitement that had obtained in Shelton was missing here. There were no throngs of laborers, no railroad rumors to be whispered, no skinners cracking their whips over six-horse teams. The street was nearly deserted, and lighted only by the glow of lamps filtering through the windows of resorts—the meeting places of the scant population. The prairie wind breathed in the foliage of the cottonwoods that arched their branches over the houses.

But appearances are truly deceiving, and Brent knew that the quiet town was often the scene of high play, that men of the range swarmed in it after the round-ups and the beef shipment, that there was money there—and influence.

As they approached the bank building Brent smiled to himself. It was James Lynch who owned the bank and the Rabbit Foot Ranch. It was he who had paid half the reward money Brent had collected for breaking up the band of rustlers who had stolen Rabbit Foot cattle. But the greatest thrill Brent had received here had been through his few meetings with Carol Lynch, the banker's niece. It was Carol who had called him "The Outlaw Samaritan"; who had trusted him when all others were suspicious of him, he thought. It was of Carol Lynch he was now thinking.

Therefore, when they reached the little walk leading back from the bank to the Lynch home, he was startled when a feminine figure appeared.

The girl appeared startled, too. She stared at Brent and the boy in the faint light and slowly smiled.

"I thought you would repent, Mr. Brent," she said with a little laugh.

"That starts me guessing," said Brent, removing his hat.

"Haven't you returned in hopes I'll give another party?" she mocked.

"I'm right sorry, ma'am, that I couldn't stay to the last one," he retorted gallantly.

"Well, uncle isn't," she said, laughing. "He might have lost a lot of stock if you hadn't left that night and caught the rustlers. Cattle mean money to uncle, and you know uncle thinks quite well of money."

"We all do, don't we, ma'am?" said Brent.

Alan had taken off his hat and the girl shook hands with him.

"What do you think of your adopted father?" she asked the boy.

"He's my pardner," answered the boy gravely.

The girl looked quickly at Brent. "I wonder which of you is in the making," she said whimsically. "Are you making the boy wild, Mr. Samaritan, or is he taming you?"

"I reckon you've got me tame, Miss Carol," answered Brent.

She lifted her brows. "I—because I—" She flushed and bit her lip. "I must assume that you are also a prairie cavalier, Mr. Brent?"

"Just what is that, Miss Carol?" Brent inquired in his drawl.

"I'm sure I don't know," she said. "What brought you back here?"

Brent waved an arm. "You're plumb full of questions, Miss Carol. Let me ask one. How is your uncle?"

"The same," she answered, laughing. "Haven't you called on him yet? But I know you haven't, or he would have told me. He was interested in you, Mr. Brent."

"He had to be," Brent said with a grin. "But I don't think he likes me," he added soberly.

"He just can't make you out," the girl explained. "You don't give anyone a chance to get acquainted with you, do you?"

"We cavaliers are peculiar," Brent evaded.

The girl's laugh rippled on the still air. Behind them, up the walk, a door opened and a shaft of lamplight struck through the darkness.

"Are you out there, Carol?" called a man's voice.

"Coming, uncle," she replied. Then to Brent in an undertone: "Would you like to come in and see my uncle?"

"Not to-night, Miss Carol, thank you. I haven't any business with your uncle. Some time I might call on you—"

But she was hurrying up the walk. Brent saw her figure for a moment in the light in the doorway, and then the darkness closed in.

They started on down the street. Alan put a hand on Brent's arm. "You like her, Steve?" he asked.

Brent looked at him in surprise. "Now it's you that's gettin' the question habit, young fellow; I'm goin' to put you to bed!"

"Where, Steve?"

"In the hotel. An' don't you leave the room till I come for you, if it's a week."

They crossed the street toward the hotel.

"Will I get my gun back, Steve?" the boy asked anxiously.

"That's a fair question, son. Yes, I reckon you will."

"Steve, how did the sheriff come to let us out—just because he knows us?"

"Boy, it's been ten years since I gave up tryin' to figure out the workings of a sheriff's mind," said Brent. "But Ed Furness is no fool."

They entered the hotel where Brent spoke a few words in an aside to the clerk. The clerk then showed them to a room upstairs without asking them to register. He left them, and Brent waited until the boy was in bed. As he prepared to blow out the light, Brent said:

"Get a good sleep. I'll try not to wake you up when I come in."

Alan winked at him from his pillow. "I believe you *do* like her, Steve."

The next moment the room was in darkness, and Brent was closing the door. He met Sheriff Ed Furness on the steps in front of the hotel.

"Put the youngster to bed?" asked Furness.

Brent nodded. He did not appear anxious to talk with Furness, but the latter apparently had something on his mind.

"How much do you know about this business up at Shelton, Brent?"

"That depends, Sheriff. I might know a lot an' I might be kiddin' myself."

"Playing another of your hunches, I suppose?" Furness suggested.

"I've never had one fall down on me yet," Brent returned.

"You used to spring big words on me," observed the sheriff. "How many of those words did you say you had—twenty, or so? Have you got a word to fit this latest—ah—complication?"

"Shore," answered Brent. " 'Discretion' ain't a bad word, Sheriff."

"That's according to how you use it," said Furness, frowning. "You know Smith 'expects' to take you back to Shelton in the morning?"

"I do," Brent affirmed. "But expects is another slippery word, Ed."

"Where are you going to-night?" demanded Furness.

"I'll nose aroun' a bit. And, say, Ed, I don't want to hurt your feelings none, but I'd rather we kept sort of apart. Your star shines clear through your coat!"

"I'm turning in. But listen, Brent; I'm watching you."

"A man's just naturally got to be suspicious to make a good sheriff," said Brent.

Sheriff Furness went in the hotel wondering if that remark betokened satire or implied a compliment.

Brent walked back up the street. He hadn't proceeded far before he learned, with a suddenness that was almost disconcerting, that at least a portion of the information he had received from the hotel clerk was faulty. He had been told that the members of the posse were in their rooms. But as he stepped aside to avoid colliding with a man who hurried out of a resort, he found himself face to face with Smith.

The deputy's eyes widened and his jaw dropped. Then an alert light came into his eyes.

"You got out!" he exclaimed.

"Shore," said Brent, watching the man narrowly. "Why not?"

The other recovered from his surprise speedily, looked hastily around, and stepped back a pace.

In that instant Brent's right hand moved like a flash. His gun seemed to leap from its holster as if it had been dealt a blow from beneath. The cold end of the muzzle pressed against Smith's ribs, and Brent's eyes bored into those of the startled deputy.

"You heard me agree to stay in town to-night, didn't you, Smith?" Brent's words came in icy tones. "You thought it was a joke, eh? Well, it isn't a joke, Smith. I'm stayin' all right, an' I'll see you in the morning. But, remember this: If I run into you again to-night, I'll draw on sight!"

The deputy's jaw dropped again, and a look of frightened wonder replaced his startled stare.

"You're threatening me after—did you get bail, or—"

"You don't know what you're talkin' about, Smith. But there's one thing you do know. You know I'm tellin' you the truth. The sheriff's down at the hotel. You're safer there, too, than on the street, unless you keep out of my way."

Brent's gun seemed to snap back into its holster of its own accord. Smith remembered that he hadn't been conscious of the other's draw, until he had felt the muzzle of the pistol against him. It was the fastest demonstration of gun manipulation that he had ever known. He stepped back.

"Are we quits for to-night?" Brent asked sharply.

Smith's eyes narrowed as he drew a quick breath. "We'll call it that," he said with a dark look.

Brent stood watching him as he went down the street in the direction of the hotel.

CHAPTER TWENTY-THREE
A Rescue and a Refusal

Brent waited in the shadow near the wall of the building until Smith had disappeared. His lips were tightly pressed, his eyes cold and hard. It seemed as though the indecision of the last few days had left him. When he again turned up the street there was more spring in his step. He lifted his face to the stars and drew a deep breath.

One by one the resorts were inspected by him through the grimy windows. He entered none of them and finally came to a halt near the bank building. He rolled a cigarette, lighted it, and inhaled deeply. He frowned as though disappointed.

"Not here yet," he muttered to himself. "I wonder if my hunch has gone back on me."

The street was now nearly dark. Only the dim light from the hotel windows shone. There were three buildings on that side of the street below the bank, and they were dark. The door of the hotel opened and a man came out upon the little porch in his shirt sleeves. It was the clerk. Brent saw him look up the street and go back into the hotel. There seemed nothing unusual in the incident.

Brent's right hand paused in the act of raising the cigarette to his lips. He cocked his head and listened. Faint, rhythmical sounds came to his ear from west of town—the measured beat of hoofs.

He listened for a few moments and, tossing away his weed, crossed the street above the hotel. He started toward the hotel and reached a dark spot where there was an opening between two buildings. He had barely turned his head toward the opening through natural caution when dark forms came hurtling out of the space. His leap backward and the dart of his hand to his gun were as a single motion, but it availed him nothing. One of the men literally fell into his arms, knocking down the gun; the others closed in.

Brent brought the barrel of his weapon crashing against a head, but in another moment two pairs of hands had gripped his arm. The gun was wrested from his grasp. He fought off the man who had run into him, dealt him a blow with his left, and kicked as best he could at the one who had attempted to seize him about the waist.

But his assailants were not weak nor inexperienced in a rough-and-tumble fight. Brent had no doubt but that they were the members of the posse whom Smith had recruited when he returned to the hotel. They doubtless had crept down the back stairs and out the rear door to take up their position in ambush. The action of the hotel clerk in coming out on the porch to look up the street took on a certain significance. These deductions flashed through Brent's brain almost in an instant.

Next moment he was wrestling with the two men who had grasped his right arm while others attacked him from behind. They were in the street by now; but the street was deserted. Then, above the scuffle of feet and the heavy breathing, Brent heard the pound of hoofs.

He succeeded in freeing himself from the pair in front, but as he did so he felt an arm clamp under his chin, and he was jerked backward with cruel force. He stumbled and went down, falling upon a yielding body. The others came down upon him, and he was held fast while the man under him cried out.

There were shouts, and the load on Brent's chest shifted. He threw off another man and scrambled to his feet in time to see a big man flinging two of his assailants aside. Two others fell in with the newcomer, and Brent saw three horses with empty saddles standing near.

"Half a dozen on one, eh?" the newcomer was saying. "Some scrap!"

Brent started as he recognized the voice and figure of Snag Dorgan.

The clerk had come out of the hotel and was standing on the porch. Someone seized Brent's left arm and spoke to Dorgan.

"Who are you?" It was Smith.

"That ain't the question," said Dorgan, looking queerly at Brent in the faint light. "What are you gents piling six to one on this fellow for?"

"I'm an officer," said Smith hotly, "and this man is an escaped prisoner."

Brent whirled with a suddenness that freed him from Smith's grasp. He sent his right crashing to the deputy's jaw, and the man went down in a heap. Brent swung on a second man, driving home his powerful left, leaped over Smith, and gained the shadow near the space between the buildings. His foot struck a hard object, and he quickly picked up his gun.

"Stay where you are!" he warned them.

Smith was slowly getting to his feet, dazed. The others, momentarily leaderless, cowed by Brent's command and the presence of Dorgan and his two companions, remained motionless.

Smith swore roundly. "Where'd you come from?" he fairly shouted at Dorgan.

"We just rode in from the ranch," said Dorgan in mild tones. "How'd we know you was an officer an' that that man was a prisoner? Looked to us like a mighty one-sided scrap. How do I know you're an officer?"

"You don't, you big fool!" cried Smith, his voice wild with rage. "Now he's beat it again."

"You didn't make much progress with him when you had him," said Dorgan with a short laugh as he turned to his horse.

Brent slipped away in the darkness to the rear of the buildings, found his way to the back of the hotel, and entered. He stole up the stairs to the room where he had left the boy. He found Alan asleep. He locked the door, propped a chair under the knob as an extra precaution, took off his boots, hat and gun belt, and lay down beside the boy.

He was awake with the dawn and arose imme-di-ately. As he was pulling on his boots, Alan awoke. Brent waited while the boy washed and dressed, and the two went quietly down the rear stairs. They made their way to the barn behind the hotel where Smith had put up the horses. The barn man was stirring, and Brent ordered their horses saddled. The barn man, who knew them both, readily complied, and Brent and the boy rode out the rear of the barn into the cottonwoods along the stream that flowed slowly through the town.

They dismounted in a small meadow formed by a bend in the creek about a mile downstream, removed the saddles from the horses, and picketed them by the lariats that they carried with them. Then they walked back to town.

One of the small cafés was open, and they went in to breakfast. When they came out the sun was up and people were on the street. Brent led the way around the rear of the buildings on the street to the hotel and entered through the kitchen. There he learned that Sheriff Furness, Smith, and the others were eating breakfast in the dining room. Brent took the boy upstairs, and they waited in their room until Brent, watching at the window, saw the sheriff and the members of the posse leave the hotel and walk down the street toward the jail, which was at the lower end of town.

"Let me do any talkin' that's to be done," Brent cautioned the boy as they left the room and went down.

A few minutes later they entered the sheriff's office to find him sitting at his desk and Smith and his men sitting in chairs about the room. Smith looked at Brent with mingled surprise and wrath. He rose at once.

"Well, I guess I better be starting, Sheriff," he said in a businesslike tone. "I'll send a man for our horses."

The sheriff looked at Brent. "Ready to go?" he asked casually.

"I'd like to have a little talk with you, Sheriff," said Brent. "We'll have time while the man gets their hosses."

The sheriff rose leisurely and motioned to Brent to accompany him into the cell room. He shut the door after them.

"Another stall, but it won't do him any good," said Smith. "Go get the horses some of you fellows—no, wait. Go have 'em saddled, one of you. We can ride out from the barn."

One of the men left, and Smith turned to Alan, who was standing apart from them by the sheriff's desk. Out of the corner of his eye the boy could see his belt, holster, and gun still lying on the desk.

"Say, boy, how old are you?" Smith asked sternly.

"Ask Steve," replied Alan quickly.

Smith's face darkened. "You'll talk when you get to Shelton," he said savagely. "If you'll take a tip from me, you'll tell all you know." His tone became confidential. "If you do that, young fellow, the judge will let you off. I can promise you that. You don't want to go to prison, do you?"

"I'll go if Steve does," was the ready reply.

"Listen to me," said Smith sharply, stepping toward the boy, "you'll change your mind—"

Alan had gone swiftly around the desk. His hand fell quickly on the butt of the gun on the desk, and his eyes flashed.

Smith stopped, thunderstruck. Then the boy's hand drew away from the gun, and he smiled.

"What was you goin' to say, Mr. Smith?"

The deputy swore as the door to the cell room opened and the sheriff and Brent came in. Brent took in the situation at a glance, and looked at Alan. The boy winked deliberately.

"He's been asking questions," he said, with a nod at Smith.

Brent turned to the sheriff with a grin. "Maybe you'll answer 'em," he suggested.

At this moment the front door burst open and the man who had gone to order the horses saddled appeared.

"Two of the horses are gone!" he exclaimed.

Sheriff Furness held up a hand. "All this isn't important," he said addressing Smith. "As I understand it, you want to take these two back to Shelton because, as you say, they ran away from you yesterday."

"Because they're suspected of robbing the bank up there," said Smith angrily.

"But you didn't see them do it," the sheriff pointed out. "You've found nothing on them, although this Brent has a money belt on that you overlooked. But he seems to have got that money honestly. I don't see that you've got much to go on, Smith."

"I've got this much," was the hot retort. "I captured them, an' they're my prisoners; I'm going to take them along."

The sheriff beckoned to Alan and then ushered the boy and Brent into the cell room. Once again the barred door clanged shut after them, and the sheriff turned the key in the door of the center cell.

Smith watched with a look of astonishment as Furness pocketed the key.

"What does all this mean?" he demanded.

"You brought them here an' left them with me, an' I propose to keep them," replied the sheriff smartly as he brushed past the deputy.

"You can't do that!" stormed Smith. "It isn't law, it isn't—"

"But I'm going to do it!" thundered Furness, whirling on the other. "You tell Sheriff Neil up there that I have these two down here and if he wants them, to come after them himself an' to bring a warrant!"

"You're after the reward!" shouted Smith in a rage. "You're tryin' to beat us out of it! You think you can get it when we caught 'em? You—" He ceased shouting as he saw the look in Sheriff Furness's eyes.

"There's no use making a row," said Furness evenly. "You won't get 'em. You can start north any time, but don't forget to give my message to Neil."

Smith took a final look at the pair in the cell. His fists clenched, and he swore inarticulately. Then he motioned to his men to leave, and, with a fierce glare at Furness, stamped out after them, his face white with rage.

Sheriff Furness stood in the outer doorway of the jail until he saw the posse ride out of town at a thundering gallop. Then he calmly unlocked the cell door and freed Brent and Alan. They followed him into his little office.

Brent gathered up the boy's belt and gun, gave them to Alan, and leaned on the desk. He eyed the sheriff with an amiable grin as that official sat down in his chair and looked at the two of them quizzically.

"I'm still half guessing," said Furness finally. "You two get out of here!"

CHAPTER TWENTY-FOUR
"You're the Doctor"

Brent continued in a thoughtful mood as they walked to the hotel. He had learned that Smith had said nothing of the events of the night before. It was plain that the deputy from the north had assumed that Dorgan and his companions were from some neighboring ranch. It was just as well. But Dorgan's interference in the fight bothered Brent nevertheless. Dorgan had undoubtedly saved him from being hustled out of town and up to Shelton; for Smith must have suspected something the night before, and his speedy departure that morning, after but little argument with Furness, proved it. Therefore Brent felt that his freedom and presence in town were due to Dorgan.

When they entered the hotel the first man he saw was the very man he was thinking about. Dorgan was sitting in a chair in the little lobby which was otherwise deserted. He grinned at Brent amiably. Brent told Alan to go up to the room and wait for him, and when the boy had gone he sat down in a chair beside Dorgan.

"They didn't get you, eh?" said Dorgan in a way that showed he knew all about it, or at least enough of the details to form an opinion.

"No," said Brent, frowning slightly. "But I reckon they would have had me last night if it hadn't been for you."

Dorgan nodded, took out a huge cigar, and lighted it. When he offered a smoke to Brent the latter declined and brought out his tobacco and papers.

"Reckon you must have some kind of a pull down here," Dorgan observed.

"That outfit didn't have anything on me," Brent evaded.

"Oh, they could have made it tough for you for a while," said Dorgan.

"Maybe so, maybe not. Anyway, you know I spoke the truth when I told you that posse was breezin' down."

"I wasn't scared none," said Dorgan dryly.

The absolute frankness of the man, although it was indirect in what it implied, was not lost on Brent. His brows knitted.

"I'd almost rather you hadn't took a hand in that affair last night, Dorgan," he said slowly.

"You don't have to feel under obligations," said Dorgan genially, but giving Brent a shrewd look. "You tipped us off about the posse." He indulged in a chuckle. "How come they didn't take you back this morning?"

Brent frowned more deeply. "They didn't have as much on me as they thought, but I hope you're getting me right, Dorgan."

The big man leaned toward him. "You mean you've finished with your thinking?" he said meaningly. "It's all right with me. You figure on making any announcements here?"

"You ain't figurin' on stayin' here long, are you?" asked Brent, lifting his brows.

"That doesn't answer my question," said Dorgan, his eyes narrowing.

"You want a show-down," said Brent, looking at him steadily. "I reckon you're entitled to it, Dorgan. I'm not traveling with you one way or the other for what you want."

"An' you're not answering the question," said Dorgan with a faint sneer.

"Not as long as there's no more need for answerin' it than now," was Brent's cool reply.

Dorgan's eyes flashed. "You're the doctor—an' you're treating your own case. That fair enough?"

"You busted in on me, Dorgan," Brent drawled out. "I wasn't lookin' for you as I can remember."

Dorgan got to his feet. His holstered gun was on a line with Brent's eyes as he towered above him. His hand dropped lightly to its butt.

"It's always good to know how we stack up," he said with an evil smile.

"That occurred to me soon as I saw you this morning," Brent returned.

"If I was you," and Dorgan looked about the lobby casually, "I'd hit back for that cabin of yours an' the kid's."

Brent rose with alacrity. "I wouldn't be surprised if I had to doctor my case right here, Dorgan."

Dorgan waved his cigar. His small black eyes gleamed viciously.

"I might need help curing it," he said, and swung on his heel with an ugly laugh.

Brent watched him go and then climbed the stairs slowly. His face was grim, but when he entered the room and saw Alan's eager look, he smiled.

"Come on, son," he said cheerfully. "Bring your belongings. I'm goin' to put you up in better quarters."

As the boy got his gun belt, weapon, and a few other possessions together, Brent stood looking out the window. He shook a forefinger at the lad as he opened the door.

"I want you to keep a check rein on that tongue of yours, young fellow; now remember that!" He scowled, but there was a suggestion of a twinkle in his eyes, and the boy smiled up at him.

Brent led the way downstairs, out of the hotel, and by a roundabout way to the Lynch home behind the bank, where he knocked at a side door.

It was opened by the person he was looking for, and he swept his hat low.

"Mornin', Miss Carol. Can I have a few words with you?"

"Of course," said the girl, stepping back from the door. "Come in."

They entered a small living room and Carol motioned them to chairs.

"Miss Carol," said Brent when they were seated, "I reckon you're a more or less obligin' person."

"Why—thank you," said the girl, lifting her brows in surprise.

"Yes, I reckon you are," Brent continued. "An' I guess you wouldn't want a future president of the United States, or a future first-class cow hand, to—er—suffer for want of proper—er—companionship at a right pertinent time when—"

"Now, Mr. Brent!" Carol broke in. "You are referring to Alan, I know. Why not come right to the point without distributing a lot of that language you are capable of—unless this is a purely early morning social call."

Brent grinned. "It *is* a bit early for a social call, Miss Carol. No, this isn't any such thing. An' I do happen to be referring to this young ruffian here." He scowled at Alan with mock severity. "He has the makings of a bad man, or a president, in him, I reckon, an' I think enough of him to want to see him in powerful good hands for a spell."

"You wish to leave him here?" said Carol, looking at Alan's serious face with interest. "Are you going away for a time, Mr. Brent?"

"That I don't know, ma'am. Mebbe so, mebbe not. But something might come up that I'd have to move so—er—fast that Alan might not be able to catch up. You see?"

The girl looked squarely into his eyes, plainly questioning.

Brent shook his head slightly. "Don't know anything but that, Miss Carol. But I would like to leave Alan where I know he's safe—an' in the best of hands."

Alan smiled broadly at the girl. "He means you, ma'am."

Carol flushed slightly, looked at him gravely, while Brent glared at the boy, genuinely irritated.

"I haven't been able to teach him to keep his mouth—to keep still till he's spoken to, ma'am," said Brent, trying in vain to catch the boy's eye.

Carol laughed. "Well, Mr. Brent, I *am* interested in this young man, and enough so to take him in and look after him until you—you—become more settled."

"That would be mighty fine of you, Miss Carol. Will you behave if you stay here, young fellow?"

"You know I will," said Alan, favoring him with a grin as Brent scowled.

"If you don't I'll just naturally rope you an' drag you across Blizzard Bench!" Brent warned him. Then, to the girl: "Had I better see your uncle about this?"

"No need of that," Carol replied. "I know in advance that he won't object."

"Then I'll be goin'," said Brent, rising.

When he reached the door, Alan called to him. "You're sure coming back, Steve?"

Brent opened the door and shot him a kindling glance. "I shore hope to, son."

Carol followed him out, leaving the boy inside. "Is there anything in the wind, Mr. Brent?"

"There is, ma'am," he drawled out in reply. "There's a hint of fall. I look for an early fall an' a long Indian summer; a short, hard winter, and an early spring." The brim of his hat touched the steps as he bowed low.

"You cavaliers are all fair-weather men," she said in a superior tone.

"We have to be that," Brent answered, grinning. "Our business requires it, ma'am."

As he departed, she looked after him with an amused light in her eyes; then she smiled and went inside.

Brent went straight to the bank. He walked without ceremony into the office of Lynch, the banker, nodded to that astonished gentleman, put his hat on his desk, and sat down in a chair across from him.

"You've got the nerve of a—a—"

"Money changer," Brent interrupted, leaning on the desk. "It isn't such a bad thing to have. If I hadn't had some of it—well, you know." He nodded significantly.

"I don't suppose I'll ever hear the last of your catching that rustling outfit out to my ranch," the banker grumbled. "Did you come back to deposit that reward money you got away with?" he added in a more respectful tone.

"Not to-day. Little later, maybe. This might not be a good time to have a few thousand cash in here, Lynch. Cash, I mean."

"What are you getting at?" the banker demanded. "Let's have it."

"They knocked off the bank up in Shelton the other night. Got plenty an' got clean away."

Lynch looked at him thoughtfully, shrewdly.

"You mean, say, for instance—the men who did it might be headed this way?"

"Bank robbers have been known to travel long distances between jobs," Brent drawled out. "An' then again, they've been known to stop on the way. They got it over the counter up there."

"I don't keep much out front," answered Lynch, frowning.

"An' your safe ain't such a powerful strong contraption," said Brent.

"Are you giving me a warning?" asked Lynch quickly.

"Maybe I'm kiddin' you," said Brent, with a different look in his eyes as he picked up his hat and rose briskly. "Fine day, Mr. Lynch. I wouldn't feel right if I came to town an' didn't visit you. So long."

"Just a minute," said Lynch sharply. "Did you just come from Shelton?"

"Why, now that I think of it, I did."

"Then what do you know about it?" asked the banker, rising.

"I know it was a clean-cut job by men who meant business," replied Brent. "They might have lit out for the Canadian line; an' they might have come south. That's all."

He left Lynch standing by the desk, frowning thoughtfully.

As he came out of the bank he met Snag Dorgan for the second time that morning.

"Making a loan?" Dorgan inquired.

"Might be makin' a deposit," Brent returned.

"I had you figured as a money-maker," Dorgan said with a searching look.

"Thanks for the compliment," said Brent with a wry smile. "Nice day."

Dorgan scowled after him as Brent sauntered up the street. Then Dorgan himself entered the bank.

Brent, watching furtively, saw him go into the bank, and waited out of sight until he came out looking into a bank book he held in his hand.

"So he's made a deposit," muttered Brent to himself. "An' it took him more'n half an hour to do it. A man can learn a lot about the inside of a bank in that time."

CHAPTER TWENTY-FIVE
Under Cover of Darkness

After going for the horses and returning them to the barn, Brent frequented the resorts during the day and early evening. He saw Dorgan, Royce, and Snally later in the morning, but they rode away shortly after noon, going westward. Brent visited the bank hurriedly and learned from the man in the cage, whom he knew, that Dorgan had deposited a thousand dollars and that he had talked with Lynch, telling him he and his two friends had been offered jobs at the Rabbit Foot and that they were going out to go to work.

"Whew!" thought Brent as he went out. "Depositing money in Lynch's bank an' takin' jobs on his ranch. That deposit must have convinced Lynch. He likes money, an' his brains are controlled by it."

That evening he sauntered to the sheriff's office and talked a while with Ed Furness. When he left, Furness thoughtfully tapped the top of his desk for a spell and then made his way to the post office in the general store, where he talked with the postmaster, a man who was a volunteer deputy.

Brent visited Alan for a few minutes at the Lynch home. The banker came in, but Carol was there with Brent and the boy, so he forbore asking any questions and soon left them.

During the next two days Brent, to all appearances, was enjoying a quiet rest in town, after the manner of a sensible cow hand who appreciates a rest when he can get it and who is careful with his money.

Then came a day of lowering clouds that thickened in the late afternoon, with a black curtain sweeping down from the mountains in the northwest. It grew dark, and a strong wind whistled in the cottonwoods and sent branches scurrying down the street in the whirling clouds of dust. Livid streaks cut the black curtain, and the artillery of the storm was unleashed. The rain fell in a solid, gray wall, hurled across the prairie by a wind of nearly hurricane velocity. Night had fallen when the air cleared of rain, and the storm went rumbling away in the southeast. But it was a night of intense blackness, for the storm had left a veil of gray clouds in its wake as a possible signal that more was to come.

Brent went to the hotel early for supper, and after he had eaten he went upstairs to change his clothes. The wind was cold and called for wool to shut it out. Brent intended to be out this night.

At the Lynch home, Alan, who had become a favorite with all, was busily engaged in chopping a branch that had been torn from a tree and thrown upon the rear porch. He was working by the light of a pair of lanterns. Carol had come out to watch him; for he handled an ax with the skill of a woodsman. It was pleasing to watch the graceful movements of his body; to note the thoroughness with which he attended to his task.

Suddenly from the darkness at the rear of the house there came a hail.

"Hey, Alan; Brent wants to see you."

The boy let the ax down and turned eagerly. "Who're you?" he called.

He started down the steps. The form of a horse was seen in the feeble, outer ring of light from the lanterns.

"Come back, Alan, till you know who it is," Carol cried in warning.

But the warning came just as a form leaped out of the darkness and seized the boy, who struggled lustily but unsuccessfully as he was carried back into the darkness.

Carol screamed. Her uncle and the cook came running out as the girl hurried down the steps with a lantern, calling for Alan. Lynch ran back in the house and came out with a rifle. They searched all about the house; but there was no sign of the horse, the mysterious rider, or the boy.

Carol started down the walk from the house at a run.

"Where are you going?" her uncle shouted.

"I'm going for Steve!" she called back over her shoulder.

When she reached the street she paused for a few moments. Where would she be most likely to find Brent? It was early, but too late for him to be at dinner. Some resort? Most likely. Or the hotel? There were several resorts, and it would take time to visit them all. But there was only one hotel. She decided to try the hotel first.

She ran across the street, slipping in the mud, wetting her feet in the few pools of water, splashing her clothes. When she had almost gained the sidewalk on the opposite side her feet flew from under her and she fell in a pool of water, the lantern flying from her grasp to crash against a stone and go out. She struggled to her feet. Her dress was covered with mud; it was on her hands and face, in her hair.

She reached the walk and staggered to the hotel, up the steps, into the lobby.

"Brent!" she gasped out at the desk. "Is he here?"

"I—think—he's upstairs," stammered the astonished clerk. "Room sixteen in the front. Shall I send for him?"

For answer the girl ran to the stairway, her clothes dripping, her shoes leaving a muddy trail the length of the lobby.

She found the room and knocked loudly. There was no answer, and she was about to knock and cry out when the door was opened unexpectedly by Brent who stood to one side, his hand on his gun.

"Steve!" she cried. "Mr. Brent—they've kidnapped him—he's gone!"

"Where have you been?" he said, staring at her stupidly.

For a moment she recalled what her appearance must be like; then she remembered her mission.

"Steve Brent, don't talk about me—don't look at me. Alan was out on the porch chopping off a branch when a man called to him that you wanted him. He ran down the steps and they grabbed him and carried him off. He's gone, I tell you he's kidnapped!"

Brent was now alert enough. He asked no more questions.

"Didn't figure they'd get started so early," he said to himself as he hurriedly got his hat and threw on a coat. He blew out the light and, taking her by the arm, escorted her quickly downstairs.

"Have my hoss saddled right away," he directed the clerk as they went out.

"You don't have to help me home," the girl said. "You don't want to lose any time."

"You've got the right kind of pluck," he told her. Then he lifted her in his arms and carried her across the street. "I want to see the hosses' tracks," he said as he put her down. He led the way to the house, where Lynch was standing on the porch with a lantern.

"Give me that," Brent commanded, taking the lantern from the banker's grasp.

He hurried around the house, with the banker and Carol following him. He speedily found the tracks of a horse and followed them west of the house to where they led up a path between the trees to the open prairie. He went back, gave the lantern to Lynch, and spoke sharply.

"Get word to the sheriff, but tell him I said to stay here. Remember, I said to stay here."

He ran to the hotel barn, found the clerk had sent word to the barn man, and that his horse was saddled and ready. He mounted and rode out of town at a gallop, circling around the trees to where the trail the kidnappers had taken came out upon the prairie.

It was very dark, but he could dimly see the way—"feel" it, as the saying goes in the cow country. He dismounted to make sure of the trail, and saw the fresh prints of the hoofs of one horse.

He swore under his breath as he swung back into the saddle.

"Only one of 'em, old hoss," he cried aloud as he gave the dun the spurs. "That means the boy's out of commission or tied. I reckon no man could carry that kid in the saddle if he had the use of his hands an' feet."

The clouds had banked, and darting tongues of lightning licked the sky. The flashes helped Brent on his way. Whoever had kidnapped Alan was making in the direction of the Rabbit Butte bad lands and the Carman cabin.

As Brent became convinced of this, he wondered. Who was carrying the boy away—Dorgan? Or Royce? Brent didn't believe Snally was capable of the trick, owing to his small stature. Still, it is the thin, wiry men that are deceiving in strength as well as in brains. But why should Alan's captor take him to the cabin where the boy and Brent had been—where every foot of the ground was familiar to both of them; where he could hardly avoid inevitable capture if Brent took up his trail? And surely he must know that Brent would take his trail and follow it regardless of where it led. An illuminating thought flashed through Brent's brain. Then a singular coincidence occurred.

By means of a brilliant flash of lightning that made the prairie light as day, Brent, who was looking back by instinct rather than in the expectation of making any discovery in that direction, plainly saw a horseman riding into the trees above town. He had not spied any horseman ahead, although he knew one was there. He slowed the dun down to a fast walk and thought rapidly.

"I'm goin' to play my hunch," he said finally, "an' if it brings any harm to that lad, I'll kill every one of 'em!"

He turned about and started back to town. The storm broke with all the ferocity of the storm of the late afternoon. The lightning was almost continuous, the thunder even crashing in repeated rolls, the rain sweeping down from the north in sheets.

Brent had to ease the hard going of the dun; for the prairie was treacherous with soft, slippery gumbo mud and pools of water. He thought of the possibility of the boy being carried bound or unconscious across a saddle in the downpour, wet and very likely hurt, and his lower lip curled down from his teeth in the ferocity of his look.

"I'm bankin' that they left him in town, tied in the woods probably, an' one of 'em—most likely Snally—was leadin' me on a wild goose chase to get me out of the way." He spoke aloud in the booming fury of the storm.

It was easy to keep his direction by the white radiance of the lightning play. He made straight for the trail into the trees above the Lynch place. In a short time he reached it, and for several minutes he searched as best he could by the lightning in the trees near the trail. Then he swore and went back into the trail, examining it closely to see if a horse had left it anywhere, or if a man had dismounted along it. He couldn't make out that either of these things had happened.

He rode off the trail at its lower end and tied his horse among the trees, throwing his slicker on the saddle and the horse's flanks and securing it against the wind. Next he crept along the underbrush and stole to the rear of the Lynch house.

There were lights in the house. He knocked lightly at the rear door.

Lynch answered the summons himself, with a cocked gun in his hand. He stepped back with an exclamation of surprise when he recognized the visitor. Brent pushed past him into the kitchen, and he closed the door.

"Did you find the boy?" Lynch asked eagerly.

Brent smiled faintly, pleased at the banker's show of interest in Alan.

He shook his head. "No, I didn't find him. I don't believe they took him out of town, Lynch. I think they hid him an' one of 'em rode away to get me out of town. Maybe the tracks I saw wasn't made by the fellow who was here at all. I'm playin' that hunch."

"Why, was there more than one of them?" asked the banker, still holding the cocked gun.

"I'm not shore of that, either," replied Brent with a frown. "Put that gun away, Lynch, or you're liable to shoot your foot off."

The banker uncocked the gun. "Man I hired today for the ranch was in to ask about the business. Wanted to know where you was. Name's Dorgan; know him?"

Brent started. "He was here? Heard about him— yes. Thought he was goin' out to your ranch."

"He did—a few days ago. They came to-night for some gear they needed."

"They—more'n one?" Brent asked quickly.

"Dorgan and the little fellow—Snelly, or Swally, or some such name. What's the matter with you, Brent?"

Brent was swearing in an undertone. So Snally hadn't ridden away—and Dorgan hadn't ridden away. And Royce hadn't showed up with the others? Then it wasn't improbable that Royce had taken Alan away. He was a big man, Brent reflected, and he could handle Alan, perhaps—threaten the boy, anyway. And it would not be against Royce's principles to rap the lad on the head with his six-shooter. Yes, Royce was capable of it. And in drawing Brent away, clear to the bad lands if necessary, it wouldn't go against Royce's grain to take a pot shot at him from ambush. Dorgan wanted Brent out of the way; he had called to learn if he had taken up the chase after the boy's kidnapper.

"Where did you tell Dorgan *I* was?" Brent asked the banker.

"I told him you'd gone out after that fellow. I got your word to the sheriff, although I couldn't see why you didn't want his help. But I did as you said, for you're a queer number, and sometimes I think you know what you're doing."

"Thanks," said Brent dryly. "I take it you're beginning to trust me, an' I'm goin' to ask you to trust me a whole lot to-night. I want the keys to your bank's back door. Then I want you to go to bed, or at least to put out every light in the house."

Lynch stared, incredulous. "You—want the keys—to the bank?"

Brent nodded sternly. "An' don't forget about the lights."

"But the keys!" Lynch ejaculated. He could not appear to understand.

Brent took him by the arm. "Time's short, an' I'm goin' to let you in on my hunches. You like the boy, an' I"—his voice trembled with emotion—"I love him like a brother! This all has to do with him in a way, but it's too long to tell you everything now. I believe that this Dorgan an' Snally are goin' to try to rob your bank to-night. These two, an' another lit out of Shelton mighty quick after that bank was robbed up there. I saw 'em do the job! They tried to get me to go with them before an' afterward, but I'm not in their class. Believe me, for the boy's sake. They mustn't be scared off by any big show of force. We don't need the sheriff, yet. We need that dog-goned nerve you threw in my face to-day. Give me those keys!"

As Brent finished speaking, Carol came into the room. When she saw Brent, her eyes lighted, eager with hope.

Brent shook his head and turned back to Lynch, meeting his gaze squarely.

"You want too much," the banker mumbled as if to himself. He *did* love money. He was afraid.

"What does he want?" Carol asked, touching the banker on the arm.

"He wants me to trust him as I never trusted a man before," said Lynch slowly.

Brent opened his mouth to speak, but halted at a crash of thunder.

"*Do* it, uncle," said the girl calmly, as the fearful sound subsided.

The banker's struggle burned in his eyes as he looked at the two of them. Brent's heart bounded, and he turned his eyes, burning with pride, on the girl. Then he looked at Lynch anxiously.

"All this is takin' time."

Lynch took a deep breath, reached in his pocket, hesitated, and then handed over the keys.

CHAPTER TWENTY-SIX
A Hunch Comes True

Steve waited until the lights in the rear of the house were darkened and then left by the kitchen door. The night was black as ink, with the rain pouring, the wind slashing at the trees, thunder and lightning adding its menace to the Stygian terror. It was a night made to order for such a deed as Brent believed was planned by Dorgan and his two companions.

Dorgan had sought to allay suspicion by the deposit in the bank and by going to work on the Rabbit Foot Ranch. Also it had enabled him to get into the bank, into the rear office, to inspect the lay of the land—to learn where the vault was located, and how the building might best be entered. Everything about the bank was old-fashioned. Lynch had preferred to loan his money at good rates of interest, and keep comparatively few thousands at hand, rather than invest in a modern building and vault. But the few thousands were sufficient to attract Dorgan and the others who evidently planned a clean-up in the north country before fleeing south where they could hide for months with those who protected them.

Brent stole into the trees. He saw the lights in the house go out, one by one. The force of the storm was now abating somewhat; the lightning was less severe, and the rain was letting up. Steve, guided by the flashes, found his horse and took the dun to a point just behind the bank and there again tied the animal in the trees. He removed the slicker and tightened the cinch to avoid delay in case great haste should be necessary.

He tarried in the dense shadows, watching the rear of the bank. There was one window—the window of Lynch's private office—and the door in the rear wall. The window was barred; but the bars were old and could easily be pried loose; and the door was a common door and could easily be forced. Lynch was accustomed to enter and leave the bank at all hours through this door, and at night he did not even take the precaution to bolt and bar it on the inside and leave or enter the bank from the street. The fact that he had never been the victim of a robbery had invested him with a sense of false security.

Gradually the storm subsided; there was no more lightning, the thunder rumbled away in the south, and the rain stopped. It was about eleven o'clock when Brent stole to the rear door of the bank and made his entrance, securing the door behind him.

A faint light filtered in through the large front window from the street. By means of this, he found his way into the cage and glanced into the rear room where the vault was located. The room was in shadow, although the door into the cage was open. Lynch did not keep a lamp burning in the bank at night through fear of fire—a precaution which was a menace. When the lights in the buildings across the street were put out, the interior of the bank would be in utter darkness.

Brent looked for a place to secrete himself and found a large cabinet under the counter. It was partly filled with packages of stationery and other bank supplies. These he removed and stowed away under the counter. He found that he could get into the cabinet with room to spare. He kept low, so he could not be seen from the street, and waited patiently.

In an hour the lights across the street went out, and the bank's interior was plunged in darkness. For another hour his vigil continued, and he became uneasy. Suppose his hunch would prove to amount to nothing! Suppose Dorgan had had Alan taken in earnest with the idea of getting Brent to follow so that he could take vengeance on Brent for defying him! Suppose Dorgan had taken Alan for revenge on Brent! These thoughts bothered Brent. And Dorgan had inquired for him at the Lynch house to make sure that he had gone in pursuit. But that didn't prove much. Brent pondered whether it would not have been better to have searched the town in the first place, found Dorgan or Snally, and compelled them to go with him for the boy, or disclose his whereabouts, at the point of the gun. He had very good reasons for wanting to catch Dorgan or Snally, or both, in the act of robbing the bank—with the plunder in their hands.

Two o'clock! Would they come?

Brent heard a faint sound at the rear of the bank, and his heart leaped. He quickly and noiselessly got into the cabinet and drew the door to. Another and louder sound came—then silence. But a few moments afterward he heard sounds within the bank and knew that someone was moving stealthily toward the cage door. He pulled the door of the cabinet almost shut, leaving just enough space to hear and to see if a light should be struck.

"Cover the back window first." The voice in an undertone was Dorgan's.

Having gained entrance to the bank, after keeping an eye on it from the street, the pair felt secure within it. Brent heard them moving about less cautiously. They were covering the rear window so a light could not be seen. There was a faint glow that immediately died as Brent heard the door into the rear office close lightly. Was Dorgan in the outer office? Brent wondered. He opened the cabinet door an inch at a time. A faint glow of silver light now filtered in through the front window, and Brent smiled. The storm clouds had been driven away by the wind and the moon was out. He saw that the front part of the bank was empty.

He crept noiselessly out of the cabinet and along to the door to the rear office. Through the keyhole he saw Dorgan standing, holding a small lantern such as is used by trainmen, while Snally was slowly turning the knob of the combination dial on the door of the vault. Snally was working with his eyes on the floor and his head was cocked as if he was listening. He was operating by "feel"!

Thus Brent became acquainted with the secret of those marvelously slim, delicate fingers of the gambler. Their chief work was not to manipulate the cards in a game of chance, skilful though they were at that, but to "pick" the combinations of safes of the common type such as used by Lynch.

In a remarkably short time the door of the vault swung open. Dorgan and Snally were now eager, excited. The inner doors were opened without trouble. The third door, which was locked, was attended to with two short iron crowbars the men had brought with them. The same tools enabled them to open the cash boxes, and they crammed a sack with bills.

Brent opened the door silently and, drawing his gun, leaped to the open door of the vault.

"All right, boys, come on out! I didn't think it was goin' to be quite so easy!"

Dorgan and Snally swung about as if struck, and stared at him with bulging eyes. Dorgan held the lantern and the sack. In Snally's hands were the last few packages of bills.

"Come on," Brent invited cordially. "I told you I wouldn't make an announcement, Dorgan, if there wasn't any need of it. But there's need of it tonight in more ways than one." His eyes narrowed and gleamed dangerously as he remembered Alan Carman.

"Well, you've got us," said Dorgan. "But you had to double cross us to get us."

"No," replied Brent sternly. "I just let you double cross yourselves. Figure that out while you're stepping this way."

Dorgan advanced slowly, his eyes red with danger lights, his face dark. At the outer door of the vault he seemed to stumble, but in that instant the hand holding the lantern came up with lightning rapidity, hurling the lantern. Brent fired as the lantern struck him on the right shoulder with terrific force. It swung his right arm a bit so that his next shot spattered against the iron door of the safe.

Dorgan's heavy frame came against him, knocking him back. He fell as Dorgan fired.

"Got him!" yelled Dorgan as he leaped through the door, out the cage entrance, and through the rear door. He still carried the bag.

The lantern, being of a protected, patented type, continued to burn where it had fallen to the floor. Brent leaped to his feet. Dorgan hadn't shot him, but had thought so because he had fallen as the other had fired. Dorgan had missed him clean.

And the fall had, in turn, prevented Brent from firing and had saved Dorgan's life. But Snally was still in the safe.

"Come out of there, Snally," Brent ordered. "I'm not hit, an' if you don't come out I'll lock you in where there's not much air!"

A low moan from within the vault rewarded him. Brent peered in cautiously and saw Snally lying on the floor of the vault. He entered swiftly and found that Snally was wounded in the right side. He had been hit by the shot Brent had fired at Dorgan! But the man was conscious and stared up at him out of frightened eyes in the yellow gleam of the lantern.

Brent rose and looked down at him gravely. "Snally, you're hit an' hit bad," he said soberly. "If you get out of here right away an' to a doctor, you've got a chance. An', anyway, you're caught with the goods. There's two things I want to know. Tell me an' out you go. If you won't tell me, I'll lock you in this vault an' leave you to die!"

Terror shone in Snally's eyes. "Wha—what?" he gasped out.

"Where's that boy an' where's the plunder you got at Shelton? I've only got half a minute, Snally!"

"Royce took him—to—cabin up there. Money's —under floor."

Brent knew the man spoke the truth. He hurried out of the vault, carrying the lantern and around through the cage to the rear door just as two horses came pounding around the corner of the bank.

"That's him!" shouted a voice. "That's him, Neil. He's turning another trick!"

Brent recognized the voice of Smith, the deputy from Shelton, and also recognized the name of the Shelton sheriff mentioned by Ed Furness. They had been riding into town and had heard the shots and seen the light in the bank. Probably it was the first chance Neil had had to come down, and he happened to arrive just at the most inopportune time. Meanwhile, Dorgan was making his escape. Delay was out of the question. Brent resorted to Dorgan's tactics of a few minutes before.

As the horses came close he threw the lantern upward with all his strength. It hit one of the horses, and the animal reared in fright against the other. There was a cry of pain, and Brent knew the leg of one of the men was crushed between the horses. The men were put to it to keep their seats in the saddle as their horses reared and bolted. It gave Brent the time he needed. He dashed for the trees. The men would be sure to enter the bank to investigate, and thus find Snally. There was nothing to delay his pursuit of Dorgan. He was on his horse in a few moments, riding wildly up the trail through the trees for the starlit open spaces of prairie.

CHAPTER TWENTY-SEVEN
A Boy and Two Men

It had not been one man alone who had attacked
Alan Carman behind the Lynch house early in
the night. True, the man on the horse had caught
him up and dragged him into the impenetrable
blackness of the shadow near the trees; but there
he had been taken in hand by another, a man of
great strength and frame, and bound with his
hands behind him in a twinkling. Then he had
been thrown in the front of the saddle with the
first man behind him, steadying him, and they had
galloped away, leaving the other man, who had
been afoot, behind.

Alan had struggled with all his might against
his captors. He had been too much occupied with
this to think of crying out. He had been glad
when he brought a howl from one of the men by
sinking his strong teeth in his hand. Then, when
they had ridden away, the man in the saddle with
him had held a hand over his mouth.

Thus they had gained the prairie while Carol
and her uncle were searching about the house
with the lantern. They had ridden northwestward
at a furious pace, while the girl had gone for
Brent and while Brent was taking her home,
finding the tracks and getting his own horse.

They were mounted on a splendid animal, Alan knew. A big horse that could run as well as Alan's own. And the boy's horse could run nearly as fast as Brent's.

The boy's lower teeth pressed hard against his upper lip in his angry desperation. With his hands bound behind his back he was helpless in the saddle. It was an easy matter for the rider behind to hold him with one arm. And even if Alan could have broken away, he would certainly have been thrown, and with his horse running at that speed it would probably mean serious injury.

He knew the man behind him was a big man, and he was certain it was either Dorgan or Royce, for they were the larger men of the trio who had tormented Brent and himself. He had no enemies; they were taking him away to vent their spite on Brent. This made Alan furious. His feet were free, but he had to grip the horse's sides hard with his knees to ride easy in the saddle.

He was certain Brent would take up the chase. But they doubtless had a good start, and they were on a fast horse and a strong horse—a horse that carried double easily. His spirits drooped with the thought that Brent might not be able to catch up with them that night. Then came the determination that he would outwit his captor in some way. But first he wished to learn his identity.

He rode well, so as to cause the man behind as little trouble as possible. He would try to win him over for the time being. It was fearfully dark, lightning was playing in the north, and there were mutterings in the troubled skies. It was plain that the man was making as fast as he could for the bad lands above Rabbit Butte.

"We're going to have a storm," he said over his shoulder.

"Never mind that," growled out his captor. "Just sit tight an' keep your mouth shut an' you'll be all right. If you don't, you'll catch it right."

The boy smiled to himself. It wasn't Dorgan's voice. He couldn't forget Dorgan's voice, nor the plaintive voice of Snally. Therefore it was Royce who had spoken.

Alan had formulated a correct opinion as to Royce's make-up. He knew the man was ruthless, cruel, capable of anything. For that reason he was more afraid of Royce than either of the others. He would have to be careful in his efforts to circumvent the man and escape or get the best of him—if Brent didn't come. His heart swelled hopefully as he thought of his partner.

Two white tongues struck into the black before them and the horse leaped as the whole heavens seemed to explode in a deafening crash of thunder. Then the storm was upon them.

The rain fell suddenly in torrents, as if from some celestial cascade, as the clouds opened their floodgates. They were drenched almost in a moment. Water poured off their hats, streamed down their faces, and ran from their boots in rivulets. Lightning played over their heads, blinding them. The sharp peals of thunder became a cannonade, a roar, rending the very air about them, deafening. Then came the wind in a blast of fury that nearly robbed them of their breath; that drove the rain against them, whipping it into their faces until every drop was a stinging lash, while the Storm King laughed in ear-splitting detonations and shot his darting arrows of white death into the black curtain of the tempest.

The boy crowded back against his captor, startled, frightened, appalled at the ferocious onslaught of the storm. Royce's hold loosened. The horse shook its head uneasily, turned away from the stinging rain, and slowed its pace to a nervous canter. Alan felt Royce twist in the saddle and look behind. The man halted the horse, fumbled at first one side of the rear of the saddle, then at the other. As he bent around to the left, the butt of his gun struck against Alan's hands for an instant. It was just a touch. But in that instant Alan's mind reacted with an idea.

Then Royce had a big slicker untied. He shook it out, threw it about the boy, and shouted in his ear.

"I'll free your hands so you can hold that in front of us, but if you try any tricks I'll bust you over the head with my gun or choke you till you're black in the face—understand?"

"All right," Alan shouted back above the din.

Royce made good his promise and the boy, after rubbing his numbed hands, grasped the sides of the slicker. The wind nearly tore it from him.

"Put your hands in the sleeves," shouted Royce.

Alan did as he was told and found that this way he could hold the back of the slicker up before them, breaking the force of the driving sheets of rain.

Royce held his right hand far out to handle the reins. With his left he gathered in the skirt of the slicker on the left side. Thus they were pretty fairly protected in front, although the downpour still fell upon their heads and backs.

They started on, Royce keeping the head of the horse into the teeth of the storm with difficulty.

It was at the start of this storm that Brent had turned back when he saw the horseman near the trees above town. But the full force of it had not struck so far east. Alan could hardly remember such a storm in all his life in the bad lands.

They were forced to go slowly. The floor of the prairie was running water, gumbo patches were slippery as clear ice, mud holes were frequent.

Again Royce shouted in the boy's ear.

"You know a better way to that cabin in there?"

"Head for the high ridge north of the butte," Alan directed.

He was not surprised that Royce should be going to the cabin. He thought the man was seeking it as the nearest refuge from the storm. His brain was filled with thoughts of his plan and how he could put it into execution. His breath came quickly under the stimulus of his hopes. He was only afraid the storm would not last long enough. If it didn't, Royce might change his mind about going to the cabin.

But the storm continued. They were three hours getting to the entrance of the trail into the bad lands leading to the cabin. This was about the time that Brent received the keys to the bank from Lynch. They rode into the trail with the rain still beating against the slicker in front of them, and while the scant timber growth broke the force of it to some extent, it hurled broken twigs and short branches upon them at times. It struck them again as they entered the meadow below the cabin.

Alan had, with his left hand in the left sleeve of the slicker, succeeded in getting a grip on the empty right sleeve below his hand there. In this way he could hold the slicker and still draw his right hand out of the sleeve on that side. Royce, being behind, would dismount first. His right thigh, with his holster and gun, would come up and swing over the cantle of the saddle as he dismounted on the left. Alan's teeth again pressed hard against his upper lip. The storm had given him the freedom of his hands.

Royce reined in outside the horse shed behind the cabin. Alan gently loosened his left leg, and as Royce put his weight on the left stirrup and threw up his right foot, the boy's right hand darted down, grasped the gun, and drew it out in a swift motion Brent had taught him. He did it so quickly, so smoothly, that Royce, in the act of dismounting, with his thigh touching the cantle of the saddle anyway, was not aware of it.

"Get his bridle," Royce called as the boy slipped off the right side, throwing the slicker off on the left.

Alan stepped to the head of the horse and speedily took off the bridle, watching Royce, who was taking off the saddle. The man was more interested in getting in out of the rain at that moment than anything else.

They put saddle, saddle blanket, and bridle in the shed, and the horse went in.

"We'll feed him later," said Royce, coming out of the shed where Alan was. "You can—"

He stopped suddenly, his right hand on his empty holster.

"Go right around to the cabin, Royce," said Alan in a high key. "I've got the gun!"

Royce stared open-mouthed as the flashes of lightning, less brilliant now, gleamed dully on the blue barrel of the weapon in the boy's steady hand.

Darkness came for a moment and both of them leaped—Royce to where the boy had been standing, and Alan around the corner of the house. Alan ran to the door, which had been left unlocked, opened it with his left hand, and entered backward, keeping the gun leveled.

"If you make a rush, Royce, I'll shoot," he warned shrilly. "Get what I say!"

He caught the door inside with his left hand while Royce, fuming with futile rage, stood several paces away on the outside. Alan slammed the door shut. He knew where the matches and lamp were, and in a moment he had made a light.

"All right, Royce, you can come in."

After a few moments, during which the man debated whether there was anything else to do, he entered. There was a grin on his face, which he meant to appear amiable, but it was an evil grin. Malice shone in his eyes.

"Nice work, kid—an' my fault, so *I* can't kick," he said in a tone intended to be genial. "We'll let it go at that."

Alan was standing on the opposite side of the table from him. He had put the lamp on a shelf behind him. He didn't look much like a boy this night. His face was grim and stern beyond his years. He looked Royce squarely in the eye.

"You're not foolin' me, Royce, an' I won't take a chance. You had no business to take me away like this. I reckon I've got the law on my side if I have to shoot. But I'm goin' to shoot anyway, if you act funny before my partner comes."

Royce's simulated look of pleasantness changed to a glare of hate. His face darkened with rage.

He had seen the boy shoot Dorgan's hat in the air the first time they met. Also, he knew Brent had been teaching the boy tricks. The boy had a way of holding the gun—Royce's own gun. The man ground his teeth in a savage fury. It might have been Brent himself standing before him.

They were dripping wet and cold. Royce finally mastered his passion. "We might as well have a fire," he snarled out.

"Then you build it," said Alan. "Only be careful how you handle the wood. I might think you was goin' to try to throw a piece at me."

Royce clenched his fists and bit his lips. His eyes were darts of fire. Then he turned to the stove and very carefully built a fire.

"I'll make coffee," he growled out.

"Good idea," Alan admitted.

The boy sat on the edge of the table while Royce put the coffeepot on. It was well past midnight. The cabin was soon warm and the coffee made. Alan compelled Royce to sit by the table and he, himself, sat by the stove while they drank the steaming cups of coffee. Never for an instant did he relax his vigil on the other. In an hour his clothes were dry.

As another hour passed in silence he noted a change in Royce. The man appeared more cheerful. He gave an impression of expecting someone. It occurred to Alan that Royce was probably expecting Dorgan and Snally. He became instantly alert. A meeting *might* have been arranged for this very cabin where the men had been once before. It caused him to think.

The windows were curtained with burlap so that no one could see in. Anyone who came would have to enter by the door. If both Dorgan and Snally should come he would be up against odds that were discouraging.

"Say, Royce," he said, breaking the long silence, "are you expecting somebody here?"

"Me? Who would *I* be expecting?" Royce feigned surprise.

"I reckon you are, an' I want to tell you that if they try to break into this cabin, I'll have to let you have it so I can fight off the others without watchin' you." He moved the gun significantly.

Royce's mouth opened and his eyes widened. He looked stupefied more than surprised or angry. He wet his thick lips with his tongue and kept staring at the boy.

"I just wanted you to know," said Alan.

Time passed—an hour, two hours. The scene in the cabin was a queer one. Royce sat in his chair with an arm on the table, frowning, glaring, and looking at Alan with a puzzled expression by turns. The boy remained by the stove, which he managed to keep supplied with wood while still keeping the man covered. Both were waiting. Royce was waiting for Dorgan and Snally; Alan was waiting for Brent.

And finally the dawn shone faintly through the burlap curtains and they heard the sound of hoofs in the meadow. A horse was approaching at a gallop from the south. The eyes of the man and the boy lighted. Alan was sure it was Brent; Royce was mystified because he heard only one horse.

The boy rose. "Sit still, Royce," he said sharply. "An' remember what I said."

The horse stopped near the door, and they heard a man dismount with a curse. Royce grinned, and the face of the boy whitened. It was Dorgan. The next moment the door was kicked open unceremoniously. Alan looked and Royce leaped. But Alan was quicker, and his gun roared. A weight knocked Alan against the wall of the building and down, the gun clattering on the floor, as Royce fell forward on his face.

"You little devil, you saved me a job!"

It was Dorgan's voice, and the man chuckled.

Alan stared with bulging eyes at the still form sprawled on the cabin floor. He heard Dorgan talking and chuckling as if at a distance, dimly saw him pick up the gun. Something swelled in the boy's throat, and he felt sick. He shivered— but not with cold. His mouth was dry, and he wet his lips with a tongue that was also dry.

He watched Dorgan dully as the latter ripped up a plank in the floor and drew out a sack.

"Yes, kid, I reckon you saved me a job," Dorgan was chuckling. "I might have had to do it myself. No use going shares with a hombre that lets a kid get the drop on him. All right, son—we're goin'. Get up."

The command came sharply, and Alan obeyed. The resistance had gone from him. His partner hadn't come. He shuddered; he wanted to get away from the sight of that still form on the floor, with an arm twisted under it, and its feet under the table.

He obeyed willingly when Dorgan ordered him outside.

"Saddle that horse, kid," ordered Dorgan when they reached the shed.

Alan obeyed, as if in a daze. He realized that it was broad day, that the sky was clear, that the wind was blowing with less force, and that the sun would soon be up. But his brain was numbed. He looked down at his right hand.

"All right, kid, you're sure acting sensible. I'll see that you don't lose nothing by it. Get in that saddle an' lead me out of here by way of that long bench you fellows came down. Be spry now; ride ahead; an' don't try to kick up your heels, or I'll sure give you what you gave that ass of a Royce."

The last words caused Alan to shudder again. Something stuck in his throat. He swung into the saddle and rode swiftly across the clearing northward to the trail leading to Freezeout Bench, with Dorgan following him closely. He was fleeing from that thing in the cabin—from his own thoughts—from everything.

CHAPTER TWENTY-EIGHT
On Freezeout

The sun was up when they had climbed the trail to the southern end of Freezeout. The tableland, long and narrow, stretched like a monster, gray slab ahead; to the west, a band of green painted by the timbered slopes; in the north, the purple girdle of the distant mountains; to the eastward, the prairies covered with the gold leaf of the dazzling sunrise.

They struck out across the bench—the wind blowing steadily, but with diminishing vigor, since the rain had dried the hard earth. The going was good. Dorgan rode beside the boy, setting an easy pace, for his horse had been hard-ridden to the edge of the bad lands near Rabbit Butte. He was in a cheerful mood. He carried a saddlebag and that saddlebag was full of loot. He would let the boy guide him out of the tumbled country above the bench and then hit for Canada.

He looked approvingly at Alan. Sensible kid. He'd give him a few dollars to compensate him for the loss of his partner. He was glad he had shot Brent. He believed he had ridden too fast for the posse—if one had started out. Snally? Well, if Snally didn't have sense enough to get out and follow it was his own fault. It just made one less to divide with. And with Snally missing, he had not seen the sense in ringing Royce in on any division. But the boy had attended to that.

He smiled cheerfully as he looked over at Alan. Yes, he'd slip him a few dollars. Might take him along. No, that would be dangerous. But would it? He could put the fear of the law in the boy now that he had killed a man. He might take him along. The kid might prove useful. He could handle a gun, he was well set up physically, and a good-looking youngster, too. He could pass him off as his son. It would make him look more responsible and respectable in the eyes of the people up north across the line.

Alan rode with his face set, looking straight ahead, but seeing nothing; he hardly realized he was in the saddle. He hadn't intended to shoot Royce unless Royce had tried to attack him. It had all happened so suddenly. He had shot by instinct, although he hardly realized it. It hadn't been so hard to shoot. But afterward, when he lay on the floor where Dorgan had knocked him, close to the still form, it had been different. Then had come stunning realization. He would never forget it—never. He could not think of anything else but that. He looked dully around, and Dorgan smiled at him.

"Don't worry, kid; I'll look after you. I won't let them get you. You'll never hang while you're with me. Just keep a stiff upper lip an' leave it to me."

Dorgan smiled again as the boy turned his head. He had him—had him sure. He might, in time, even come to like the kid. Probably would. He could teach him a few tricks as well as that Brent. Couldn't be, though! Yes, they'd make a good pair. After a time he'd be able to trust the kid. That was more than could be said for Royce and Snally. Yes, they would make a good pair. He smiled in satisfaction, turned easily in his saddle, and looked back.

Alan heard a shout of surprise, an oath, and then a command.

"Get goin', kid; we've got to run for it!" yelled Dorgan as he drove in his spurs. "They're after us. Come on, we've got to hide from 'em!"

The boy's horse had surged ahead with Dorgan's. Instinctively Alan drove in his spurs. Something in Dorgan's tone and the sudden spurt of speed seemed to wake him up. He looked behind as they raced toward the north end of the bench and saw a single rider coming after them.

"Give that horse the steel!" Dorgan shouted. "There'll be more of 'em."

Alan raked his mount with the spurs, and in a moment both horses were running their best, side by side—maintaining a heartbreaking pace.

But the lone rider kept gaining and gaining fast. It seemed incredible that a horse should possess such speed. Both Dorgan and the boy kept looking back. As the rider came nearer, Alan's heart seemed to stop, then bound until it nearly choked him. His head whirled for a moment and then cleared, and a thrill shot through him. He felt every nerve tingling. And he forget everything except that the rider behind them was his partner.

"It's Steve!" he cried joyously. "It's Steve!"

Dorgan, too, had recognized the pursuer. His eyes had bulged from his head at first, and his breath had come hard. Was it his nerves? He had no nerves! But he had shot Brent down in the bank, hadn't he? Hadn't he seen him fall after he had fired? But the boy's cry proved his own eyesight. It was no ghost behind them.

Curses streamed from his lips, and he turned on the boy in savage fury.

"You ride, hear me? You ride!"

He whipped out his gun and drew down on the boy, whose joyous eyes defied him.

And now there were other riders on the bench to southward—many of them. A posse was coming behind Brent. Dorgan started to count, but desisted. What was the use? It was the man coming like the wind on a lanky, long-legged, dun-colored horse that counted. And Brent was gaining, gaining.

He was almost within range!

Dorgan rose in his saddle in an exhibition of magnificent horsemanship. He drew his gun full on the boy, and with his other hand waved Brent back.

The gesture was significant. If Brent did not give up the chase, Dorgan would shoot the boy! He was using the boy as a shield. They could run away from the posse, whose members were mounted on slower horses. It was Brent who counted, and Brent saw the signal and pulled his horse.

But Alan had seen also, and he, too, knew the significance of what Dorgan was doing. So Alan proved his measure. As the gun in Dorgan's hand dropped downward and Dorgan looked ahead for a moment, the boy deliberately threw himself from his horse. He hit the ground, rolled over and over, and lay still.

A wild cry came on the wind. Dorgan could hardly believe his eyes as to what had happened. Then he saw the dun-colored horse coming like a streak. He drove in his own spurs. But his mount was doing its utmost.

Nearer and nearer came that relentless rider. Dorgan twisted in his saddle, raised his gun, and fired. A miss! The rider came on. He fired again, and a curse died inarticulate in his throat. He could see Brent's face—and it was a face terrible to see. He raised his gun again.

The dun shot suddenly to the left. Brent's right side was toward Dorgan. Brent's gun leaped high, came down in an arc, and six sharp reports broke upon the wind. Dorgan toppled, fell from the saddle, rolled over, and came to rest face upward, while his horse ran madly on with dangling reins.

Brent completed his turn and came back to where Alan was lying on the ground. He flung himself from the saddle and, dropping down beside the boy, raised his head.

Alan's eyes opened, and he smiled up at Brent.

"I—had—to do that back there—Steve. They had me to the bad. But—I—didn't intend to—kill him, Steve. Do you believe—I did?"

"Not for a minute, son!" said Brent in a tremulous voice. "An' you didn't. You creased him over the left ear an' put him out, that's all, pardner. He'll be ready for jail by noon!"

"You're—sure, pardner?"

"Shore as anything I know—dog-gone shore, son. I looked him all over."

Then he hugged the boy in his arms as the tears came to Alan's eyes in a flood of joy.

It was this that Sheriff Furness, and Sheriff Neil, and the members of their posses saw when they came up. Sheriff Neil took off his hat, perhaps to wipe his forehead, as Furness looked about, seeing everything and seeing nothing, and swearing softly and repeatedly.

CHAPTER TWENTY-NINE
More Partners

Sheriff Ed Furness sat in his favorite chair, his feet cocked on his official desk, his cigar at its usual angle in the left corner of his mouth, and his famed derby hat on the back of his head.

Across from him, Steve Brent sprawled in a chair almost too small for him. He was rolling the customary brown-paper cigarette and performing the operation with a meticulous care which showed that his mind was elsewhere than on the simple bit of manufacturing that would yield him a smoke. The small weed finished, he lighted it and a thin spiral of smoke drifted upward into the cloud for which the sheriff's black cigar was responsible.

The door to the cell room was closed.

There was something of the manner of old friends between these two men. Yet their attitude showed that each was studying the other—with respect and curiosity.

"I'm wonderin' how you come to fasten to a derby hat, Ed," drawled out Brent.

The sheriff chuckled. "That story's sixteen years old or more'n most of 'em around here has forgot it—if they ever knew it. But I'm wondering about you, my man. Tell me something about yourself an' how you came to pick on this locality for a stamping ground, an' maybe I'll tell you about the hat."

"You're there when it comes to a bargain, Sheriff," Brent said grinning. "I don't see just why you trusted me the way you did, Ed; but we seemed to understand each other from the start."

"This last business was pretty risky," the sheriff remarked, frowning. "It's lucky you had the right hunch. You're lucky with hunches. But I took a long chance."

"Shucks, Ed!" Brent squinted at the official. "I'd have protected you. You see, when I sloped out of here with the boy I didn't know no more'n a jack rabbit where we were goin'. I only knew we were on our way. Well, I come to like the lad pretty well, but I didn't know just what to do with him, see!"

The sheriff nodded with interest.

"Dorgan made a proposition to me to hook up with him in Shelton," Brent went on. "I was almost tempted to do it. But there was the boy, an' I made up my mind it wasn't for me to hit the wrong trail. I saw them pull that robbery up there an' I knew Dorgan was clever—mighty, powerful clever. I'd heard about that hombre down south. I knew he wouldn't hit for the line where they'd all think he'd go. An' I'd heard him askin' questions about this country down here, an' this town. So I figured he'd light out for here."

The sheriff took his feet off his desk and leaned forward in his chair as Brent continued:

"I followed their tracks an' soon found they'd got enough information to know how to get into the Rabbit Butte bad lands. I found them at the Carman cabin, just where I thought they'd stop on their way through the brakes. I told Dorgan the posse was comin' to get him out of there an' into town or somewhere while I steered Smith an' his crowd off the trail. I wanted 'em to pull this job, Ed, because I thought the only way to get 'em on the other was to catch 'em pullin' the same kind of work somewhere else, see? They had nothing on 'em, an' Dorgan was too clever to carry his loot. You can see how much nerve he had when he hid the Shelton plunder right in that very cabin!"

Ed Furness had tipped his derby over his eyes, and his cigar had gone out.

"Another thing, Ed—I wanted that reward! Know why? Now don't think I'm soft, Ed, but I was goin' to put the money away to give that danged boy, Alan, something I never had myself outside of a few long words—an education. But I told Dorgan right here in town that I wasn't with him. We understood each other, an' I knew Dorgan was out to get me from that minute. When they ran off with the boy I thought they were in earnest an' were tryin' to get back at me that way. I changed my mind when I started after 'em an' saw that fellow on the horse outside of town. Then I knew it was a scheme to get me out of the picture. I told you not to follow because I had an idea they intended to rob the bank last night —an' I'd already told you what I thought was up, remember?"

"Yes, you came clean with me, Brent," the sheriff admitted. "That's why I held off."

"You know we decided to let 'em rob the bank an' beat it an' then we'd follow 'em because they'd be sure to go where the rest of the loot was. When I got back to town I talked Lynch out of the keys to the bank to get in there an' catch 'em red-handed. Any show by your office, Ed, would have scared 'em off. I thought if I could do that, I'd have 'em, an' I could make that white-livered Snally talk—tell where the boy was, first, an' then lead us to the money cache."

"Wasn't such a bad idea," the sheriff mused. "But right down risky for you."

"It worked out all right," said Brent nonchalantly. "We've got Royce an' Snally an' the loot. I suppose we'll have to split the rewards a dozen different ways—"

"No, we won't!" exclaimed Furness, slamming his fist on the desk. "You get it. I'm not a man to hand out compliments, Brent, but you did fair— you did fair, all right. Where did you say you came from?"

"Why, Ed, I don't remember sayin'," replied

263

Brent with a wide grin. Then, when he saw the sheriffs look of disappointment, he relented. "I came from down Texas way, Ed. The only parents I knew was a hoss an' a six-gun. Both of 'em has got me into trouble plumb frequent. I punched cows a lot, got tired of seein' nothing but brown hills an' mesquite an' sluggish water an' cows, so I hit for the towns."

He paused while he lighted another cigarette.

"You see, I'm not so old, Ed. I like excitement. There's others like the same thing. Down in Amarillo I got tangled up with a tough customer an'—well, Ed, if there's such a thing as a spirit, I reckon his spirit is sittin' on my shoulder now, tryin' to figure out a way to get even."

His brows lifted ever so little as he gazed squarely into Furness's eyes.

"Then I drifted north. I saw a chance to pick up a little here by workin' on that rustlin' gang, an' I did. I—I was sick of the range for a time, an' I was ready for excitement. I might even have taken a flyer at—at the kind of a game Dorgan was in, Ed. There's excitement in that game, you know. Then I met the kid, an' we got to be pardners, an' he talked me out of it without sayin' a word. Now I'm here. Of course there's still that little affair down south there, but I don't think they could make it stick. He had friends. There might be a reward, but I doubt it. They can't fix all judges—"

Sheriff Furness started in his chair, removed his hat, and put it back on his head smartly.

"Eh? What's that you said, Brent? Guess I dozed off. Didn't hear a word of it. Well, never mind—don't repeat it. I haven't got time to listen to a lot of rambling tales. You going to take a job as my deputy?"

"Nope."

"Well, then, get out of my office. I've got a great deal of work to attend to!"

Brent rose slowly. "What'd you say about that derby, Sheriff?"

Furness laughed. "I wore that hat on a bet when I was first elected," he confessed; "an' I've been scared to take it off ever since for fear it'd change my luck!"

"That all there is to it?" asked Brent incredulously.

"That's all, my boy, but—I've sort of got used to it, too."

The sunset was painting roses on a silver-satin sky. The mountains wore their royal purple robes with added luster. The sides of Rabbit Butte were draped with pink, and the foothills flung their green sashes between. The prairie wind softly whispered of the coming twilight in the waving cottonwoods.

In a room in the Lynch home, Carol, the banker, and Brent sat about a bed where Alan Carman's boyish, tanned face and chestnut hair showed in a sea of white. His left arm, in splints, lay at his side on the cover. His other arm was outstretched, and his hand in Carol's.

"So you think it was all for the good so I'd buy a good safe, do you?" the banker was asking Brent.

"I think you could make some improvements," Brent drawled out. "If I was you, I'd buy a new, burglar-proof vault, set it up somewhere, an' then build a decent building around it."

Carol and the boy laughed.

"Would you put your money in my bank if I did?" asked Lynch.

"Might. Never can tell."

"How much you got—how much will you have all told when you get this last batch of reward money?" asked Lynch curiously.

"Oh, I guess I could raise twelve thousand maybe," replied Brent coolly.

"Then why don't you put it in my bank at interest an' go out there an' take the job of being my manager on the Rabbit Foot?" demanded Lynch. "Settle down an' be somebody."

"Why, that's enough to buy a ranch of your own, Steve," said Carol.

"Or an interest in another," said Brent dryly.

"Mine!" Lynch ejaculated. "Why—why not, Brent? I believe you could make money for yourself and me, too."

"Say a third interest," Brent suggested.

The banker scowled. "For twelve thousand?" he scoffed.

"I might make money for us, as you say," Brent pointed out.

"Do as he says, uncle," advised Carol.

Lynch threw up his hands. "Oh, all right," he said as if he had been taken a mean advantage of. He rose and started out. At the door he paused long enough to say, with a smile: "I was going to suggest it myself!"

Brent got slowly up from his chair, threw his shoulders back with something of a swagger, and looked down at Alan.

"Well, I reckon we've got a home, young fellow," he said with mock severity. "An' when school starts you're shore goin' to learn something besides chasin' around the country on fast hosses, doin' circus stunts, smashing yourself up an' shootin' guns. Hear me?"

"We going to live out there, Steve?" the boy asked innocently.

"We shore are—an' for good."

"Wouldn't it be great, Steve"—and the boy's eyes lit up eagerly—"wouldn't it be great, pardner, if we had Miss Carol along?"

Brent's jaw dropped. "Well—well—of all the nervy little runts that ever—"

"You said nerve was a good thing to have, Steve; you know you've got it."

"Has he?" It was a soft, low voice.

Steve Brent looked at Carol. But she didn't meet his eyes. He stepped to her and took her arm.

"Let's go over to that sofa away from this fresh whippersnapper," he suggested. "He knows too much."

Carol rose with her eyes shining. "Does he know more than you do, Steve?"

"I reckon not," said Brent, taking her hands. "I know more than the two of you. I fell plumb head over heels in love with you, Carol, the first time you sassed me. I don't know how you feel, sweet-heart, but I figure the three of us could have a nice home out there. I know you don't love me—me bein' so unreliable an' so on—"

"Steve!" She put her arms about his neck, and he held her close as he kissed her. "I knew you were a cavalier, Steve, dear. That's why I called you one," she whispered.

"He's worse than that!" cried Alan gleefully. "He's a go-getter, that fellow!"

ABOUT THE AUTHOR

Robert J. Horton was born in Coudersport, Pennsylvania in 1889. As a very young man he traveled extensively in the American West, working for newspapers. For several years he was sports editor for the *Great Falls Tribune* in Great Falls, Montana. He began writing Western fiction for Munsey's *All-Story Weekly* magazine before becoming a regular contributor to Street & Smith's *Western Story Magazine*. By the mid 1920s, Horton was one of three authors to whom Street & Smith paid 5¢ a word—the other two being Frederick Faust, perhaps better known as Max Brand, and Robert Ormond Case. Many of Horton's serials for Street & Smith's *Western Story Magazine* were subsequently brought out as books by Chelsea House, Street & Smith's book publishing company. Although all of Horton's stories appeared under his byline in the magazine, for their book editions Chelsea House published them either as by Robert J. Horton or by James Roberts. Sometimes, as was the case with *Rovin' Redden* (Chelsea House, 1925) by James Roberts, a book would consist of three short novels that were editorially joined to form a "novel." Other times the stories were magazine serials published in book form, such as *Whispering Cañon* (Chelsea

House, 1925) by James Roberts or *The Prairie Shrine* (Chelsea House, 1924) by Robert J. Horton. It may be obvious that Chelsea House, doing a number of books a year by the same author, thought it a prudent marketing strategy to give the author more than one name. Horton's Western stories are concerned most of all with character, and it is the characters that drive the plots rather than the other way around. He died of bronchial pneumonia in 1934 at the relatively early age of forty-four. Several of his novels, after Street & Smith abandoned Chelsea House, were published only in British editions, and Robert J. Horton was not to appear at all in paperback until quite recently.

Center Point Large Print
600 Brooks Road / PO Box 1
Thorndike, ME 04986-0001, USA

(207) 568-3717

US & Canada:
1 800 929-9108
www.centerpointlargeprint.com